Hunter's Quest

The Keeper Of The Light, Volume 2

Kristen Cole

Published by Kristen Cole, 2024.

HUNTER'S QUEST

First edition. December 31, 2024.

Copyright © 2024 Kristen Cole.

ISBN: 979-8227607409

Written by Kristen Cole.

Table of Contents

To all the young dreamers who dare to embrace their unique magic, to those who fight for what they believe in, and to the unwavering love that illuminates even the darkest corners of the heart.

Prologue

Twelve-year-old Hunter Monroe lay sleeping in his bed. The house was quiet save for the slight hum of the TV from down the hallway where his father was, dozing on the couch. A street lamp illuminated the bedroom, all shades of grays and blues and greens the way most young boys' rooms were. It was homey, peaceful.

Hunter's rest was not peaceful, however, as his body twitching beneath his comforter, he watched the scenes that were unfolding behind his eyes. In his dreams, he saw a girl not much older than he, with a silver heart locket resting on her chest. The locket was detailed, ornate, reflecting sunlight in every which way as the girl strolled through an elaborate garden. Her hair–raven black–caught the sun and shimmered in a way he'd never seen before. She was so beautiful. As she giggled then, taking a step forward, then another as she fell into a run, Hunter's entire body warmed with the light she seemed to radiate.

He knew that she was not running from him. He was not in the dream, not part of the scene unfolding before him. He was simply an observer on a snippet of her life as she ran from someone he could not see, giggling and smiling and encouraging them to keep going as she wound through bushes of roses of every color–the likes of some he had never even known could truly grow. The scene was so warm, so real, he could almost feel the sun on his face.

Then the scene shifted. Suddenly, the sun was gone, replaced with a storm that raged too harshly, too closely, as the girl ran toward the manor that had been an unassuming backdrop up until now. Panic contorted the beautiful features of her face as the rain now chased her back to the houses doors, but no matter how hard she ran, no matter how close she seemed to get, she could never reach the manor doors.

The entire dream reeked of her panic, was saturated in the scent of her fear and the sounds of that storm, her panting, and her feet hitting the ground over and over and over again only to go nowhere. Hunter's chest constricted as he tried to yell out to her, to encourage her, to do anything to help her– He woke with a start, his heart racing, sweat plastering his mane of curly blond hair to his head, his body rearing to go, ready to help the girl get to her destination. It was several moments before he was able to calm himself, to remind himself that it was just a dream. Still, even after he laid down to go back to sleep, he had a hard time getting there. Every time he closed his eyes, he saw the girl: raven-black hair, the silver locket, dressed in gauzy white. And every time he saw her, he felt that horrible desperation, like she needed him , that she was in grave danger.

AFTER THAT FIRST NIGHT, the girl was featured in every dream that Hunter had. Some nights, it was that same dream as the first time, and he would wake up with the same sweating panic, that same sense of dread. In others, she simply wandered through those gardens, touching the flowers. Sometimes she was smiling; other times, she looked longingly past the edges of the garden, as if something–or someone–lay beyond them that she simply couldn't reach.

When he was eighteen, however, there was a shift. This time, the girl stood inside a manor house, having finally reached her destination. Despite this, she was obviously distressed, this time speaking to a woman sporting a slight glow about her.

"My sixteenth birthday was last week, Luna," the black-haired girl said. "What do you mean I'm now seventeen?"

The glowing woman looked down at the young girl, as if she knew much that the teenager didn't. "It is part of the curse, Syrena. You must be inside the manor by sunset or you'll age one year."

"But how is something like this possible? And why was I never informed of this before?"

"You were, child, when the curse was placed upon you."

The girl's–*Syrena's*–face twisted into a scowl. "This curse has done nothing to me but trap me in this house. My mother would never have wished something so restrictive upon me."

"Anabelle, your mother, died before she was able to complete her tasks of verifying that you were fit for the job, which is why I was forced to place this curse upon you." The other woman looked truly sympathetic, but it did nothing to ease Syrena's distress.

"So what am I to do now? What of the timeline?"

"You must still break the curse before your twenty-first."

"But now that I am seventeen–"

"You have one less year than before."

Something like fear flashed across Syrena's face as she processed the new information.

"But how am I to do such things? My mother can't help me, and my father–" Syrena choked on what could only be a sob.

"You must trust that you will know what to do when the time comes, Syrena. That is what this curse is all about." The woman reached out and placed a hand on Syrena's shoulder. "It is all a testament to you and what you will be capable of once the curse is broken." The woman smiled softly. "Have faith in yourself and all that you will accomplish, Syrena."

With that, the glowing woman vanished–and Syrena collapsed to her knees in despair.

The sound of Syrena's knees hitting the floor jolted Hunter from sleep. His heart raced as he considered all the new information that he had gathered. *A curse? Aging years in only a night?* Only a mad man would believe him if he spoke of the realism of these dreams–but he was convinced that somehow, somewhere, he was catching glimpses of a girl truly suffering through this.

Syrena.

Maybe it was the sleep deprivation, or maybe it was something else entirely, but he almost smiled at the word. He thought it again, and again, and again, as he finally named the girl he had dreamed of for the last five years of his life. He believed it to be his favorite name.

THE DREAMS CONTINUED to diversify from that point. He caught glimpses of the other people in her life, of the other places that she frequented in the manor. But he did notice that she never left—part of the curse that he understood so little about even after years of dreaming about her. Even still, he began to look forward to those dreams. Whether the girl was real, he hadn't the faintest idea, but he felt that he had some sort of claim on her, some sort of . . . connection . . . to her. More than anything, he waited for those dreams just to make sure that she was okay.

The older he got, Hunter could sense something was gravely wrong at the manor. The light that had been so vibrant in her sapphire blue eyes slowly faded over time, until shortly after her nineteenth birthday, her father passed away. Gone were Syrena's smiles and shining eyes, leaving grief and despair and longing for . . . something that Hunter could never quite decipher.

Then one night when Hunter was just cresting twenty-one and the girl was approaching twenty, he had a dream filled with terror.

Time's up. The words screeched through the dream at him, colored with panic and fear. A flitter of images, seemingly from Syrena's own mind, bombarded Hunter. He only caught glimpses—of five different shapes–a rose, a sun, a star & moon, a locket, and a cross, people he'd never seen, and of a girl that looked a lot like Syrena, sitting behind a huge glass window looking out, trapped forever.

PART ONE: THE BEFORE

Chapter One: Leaving Home

Hunter came downstairs the next morning with a bag slung over his shoulder.

His dad, Hayden, was sitting at the counter, newspaper spread out in front of him and a coffee in his hand, while his mother, Ivy, was sitting in the living room working through the morning crossword.

"Where are you off to?" his dad said as Hunter entered the room.

Hunter ignored him, grabbed some granola bars from the cabinet and threw them in his backpack. He didn't know exactly where he was going yet, but with every dream, *her* presence had grown stronger. After last night, he had felt her pull. At the very least, thanks to that pull, he knew he needed to start heading north. He hoped that as he got closer, some other hint, some other sign, some other clue, would give her away. Until then, a backpack and granola bars were the way he was going to go. Whatever it took to get to her.

The dream from the night before had shaken him to his core, chilled him, and he needed to get to her. *Now.* She was in danger.

"Hunter," his dad said more sternly when he still didn't reply a minute later. "Why are you squirreling all that food away?"

Hunter sighed. "My friends and I are going on a road trip," he lied.

But Ivy had always been able to see through him, and he heard her rise from the living room without even having to pause his rummaging.

"You're raiding our cabinets for a road trip? Those boys you call friends live off of burger grease and beer, not—" she snatched one of the bars out of his backpack and briefly looked it over, disbelief coloring every feature of her face, "—granola bars. What's really happening here?"

Hunter turned to her, pleading in his eyes. He did not want to have to explain this out loud. *Please.*

"Hunter," his dad warned again.

Hunter groaned. "I'm going after her." His hand worried the earring in his right ear, a present from his mother on his eighteenth birthday, knowing what was coming.

Ivy and Hayden shared a look, one that conveyed their confusion, and Ivy's excitement at the mention of a "her."

"I'm not following," his dad said after a moment.

Frustration roiled within Hunter, but he pressed on. "The girl from my dreams, Dad. She's real. She's in trouble. I'm . . . I'm going after her."

Shock lit his parents' faces.

"You can't be serious," his dad snapped. "You can't go chasing after someone from your dreams!" The anger in his dad's voice wore on Hunter's patience.

"I have to go. I can't explain it, but she needs me."

"We need you here," his mother said softly.

"Why does she matter more than your own family?" his dad said.

That was extreme, Hunter thought. They were acting like he wouldn't come back when whatever this was was fulfilled.

"She's a stranger, Hunter; we're your family," his dad pressed.

"She doesn't matter more than you and Mom, Dad. It's just important that I find her. I can't explain it. I just . . . I've been dreaming about her since I was twelve years old. That has to mean something, don't you think?"

"You've always had an overactive imagination," his mother added. "That's all it is. How do you know that she's even real, Hunter? Really."

"You're being impulsive," his father all but growled with disdain. "This is nonsense."

"I'm not being impulsive." Hunter's thread on his patience losing just a little more. "And, Mom, she *is* real. I can feel her. I know you don't believe me, but there is a connection between me and her. I don't know how or where I'm going to find her, but I know that I am going to do it."

"You have responsibilities here, Hunter, that can't be ignored. What about the foundation? I won't let you throw away your career for some girl we don't even know is real. A girl you met in your *dreams*." He said the last word as if it disgusted him.

"The foundation was *never* my responsibility." Hunter scowled. "You can't force me into a career that I don't even want. I can't fit into the molds that you want me to fit into... that I don't want to. I don't want to be a doctor or any of the things you want me to be, and I'm sorry for that but I just . . . it's not me, Dad. I won't do it." Hunter pressed, "I need to do this."

"You will do as you're told," his dad demanded. "You will not walk out on this family. Your place is here with us. Now put the bag down and sit for breakfast."

"I'm not *walking out*." Hunter's patience was on its absolute last thread as he hissed the words at his dad . "I'm following what I know is right. I can't keep pretending to be someone I'm not for you."

"This is ridiculous, Hunter," his mother said. "We've never asked you to be anyone other than yourself."

As his mother said that, Hunter stared at his dad, his eyes accusing him of the opposite.

"You are meant to be a doctor, just like the rest of us in this family were, generations before you," his dad said.

"Being a doctor is all you've ever wanted, Hunter," his mother continued. "Where was I when that changed?"

"It didn't change, Mom. I just stopped pretending it was what I wanted. Being a doctor was always what you and Dad wanted for me. I've never wanted it. I never wanted to be obligated to the foundation. History, exploration, *that* was always my passion. You yourself always talked about how big my imagination was. How could that be confined to something you can detail in a textbook?" Hunter finally turned to his mother. "I know you don't understand me, but I won't change who I am."

"I'm not trying to change you." Her voice broke on the sentence.

"We aren't, son," his dad seconded. "We just want to make sure that you're going to have a good career for yourself, to be able to make a living and a name, to be able to raise a family. Plus, the foundation is still growing and I'm getting older. I can't do everything by myself, and now you're telling us that you want to go off and find some girl that might not even be real? We let you have your fun, Hunter, but it's time to get serious and get smart now. No more chasing useless careers that will get you nowhere."

"See? You *are* trying to change me. You want me to be someone that I'm not. You want to push me into this perfect little box and I'm not perfect. And quite frankly, neither are you," Hunter went on, his patience gone now. "You have never believed in me, Dad. I'm tired of trying to prove myself to you. I don't want to be a doctor like you, and I never did. That's the end of it." Hunter went back to stuffing food into his backpack. "And I am *going* to save this girl."

"Then why pretend, Hunter? Why pretend to be interested in being a doctor? In being interested in the foundation? Why couldn't you just have been honest with me from the beginning? You used to talk to me, Hunter. I don't know when I lost your trust. You've changed over the last few years. It's like we're strangers now instead of family." This came from his mother.

His dad had gone silent, the way he did when his anger became all-consuming.

Hunter continued to pack as he said, "Children are supposed to change, Mom. Parents are supposed to *want* their children to change. You can't understand why I did just that, and I can't understand why you both want me to conform." He took a deep breath as he finally zipped his backpack. If he needed more food, he decided, he would buy it. "So what if the girl turns out to be fake? At least I'll have seen some of the world before I get stuck in this town, in the job that *you—*," he directed the word at his dad, "—chose for me. Isn't that at least worth something to the both of you?"

When his parents said nothing, Hunter nodded. "So when I don't comply and conform, I'm dead to you? You accuse me of walking out on you, of me thinking you mean nothing to me, but it is you two who turned your back on *me*. I want you to remember that. Especially when I do find this girl. Especially when I save her life."

With that, he slung the bag over his shoulders, secured it, and headed for the door. He didn't hear footsteps pursuing him, and though part of him was grateful for that—for not having to see the hurt on his mother's face again—another part of him reveled in it, was fueled by the silence that followed him. He made sure to slam the door just a little too hard as he left, the way that always irked them.

He'd already decided he wouldn't live with them anymore, even if this girl turned out not to be real. He wouldn't come back here, wouldn't come back to them. He deserved better than this for himself, to be surrounded by people that loved him, so he would find them, no matter what corner of the world he had to go to to do it.

HE WAS GRATEFUL THAT he had at least taken the time to pack with intention, knowing he didn't know how long he was going to be gone for. While he'd thrown food into his bag relatively haphazardly, he had the forethought to pack clothes, money he'd saved up from various jobs over the years, and a journal and paper to document anything he discovered along the way. He would be able to keep himself going for a little while, at the very least . . . save for the food situation. He did have to give his mother credit regarding the burgers and beer comment, especially as he ate his third granola bar of the day to no impact on his hunger.

Wherever you are, Syrena, he thought, *I hope you reveal it to me soon. And I hope wherever you are there is good food.*

The first few hours of travel were difficult. There were a lot of stops and switches, but sometime around eleven, he was able to settle in on the overnight commuter, which would offer an early riser breakfast if he got up early enough. He made sure to ask one of the train conductors to make sure he was awake in time for breakfast. Any free meal at this point would be a blessing to him.

That night on the train was uneventful, in both the real-world happenings and his dreams. He didn't dream of Syrena, or anything else. He woke the next morning more confused and worried than rested. He had been dreaming of her every night for years now, so not dreaming of her left him worried that something might have happened to her. But some other part of him knew that it had not. His dreams also fueled a connection between the two of them that he could not explain. Whether she felt it, understood it, or even knew he existed he wasn't sure of, but his bond with her told him that he would know if something happened to her. The thought settled his mind enough to allow him to sleep, then go get breakfast in the meal car.

The train itself was all shades of dark brown and maroon, with wood panel walls beneath big paned windows to allow him to see the country passing by. He could see the mountains in the distance, covered in trees, with the periodic dotting of lights from the surrounding towns and cities as they passed through. He had his own small cubby, with a fold down bed at head level, covered in a small mattress and a sheet and a pillow. A brown leather bench was attached to the perpendicular wall so he could sit and look out the window as he wished. A sliding door opened on the wall across from the bed, leaving one free wall to rest his pack against. This entire car was filled with identical cubicles for people to rest in, all the same shades and all carpeted to mute the sound of everyone shuffling as they readied for bed.

It was a strange experience for him. Hunter had been on the train a number of times with his family, traveling around Europe and England, but he'd never been on the train long enough to have a meal. Suddenly spending an entire night on the train, eating on it, was a new experience for him, something he found that he enjoyed. Even as nerves twinged in the back of his mind, trying to worry him about the decision he'd made, he did his best to enjoy the fact that he was, for the first time, making his own experiences for himself. Even as he did that, his hand went to his earring, working it back and forth the way he always did when his nerves got the better of him.

What was he doing? Leaving everything and heading across the country when he had never even left Sussex without his parents before?

When the thoughts crept in, he did his best to push them back, to think of the panic of Syrena in that last dream, of the danger he felt looming over her. He turned his focus back to the breakfast before him—a few slices of toast, some bacon, and a bowl of porridge, which wasn't half-bad considering it was prepared in a moving vehicle. The meal car itself wasn't that extravagant, with five or so booths on either side of a thin aisle, brown leather benches set facing white laminated tables. The paneling was the same as the resident cars, and the top part of the walls were all windows to see the landscape move past.

He did his best to focus on the scenery instead of his swirling thoughts as he finished eating. The greenery was something otherworldly, like he's stepped entirely out of England and into some mythical world–which he supposed was appropriate given the reasons for his travel. The hills ranged in size, from small and low to wide and tall the farther they got from the train, but all sported various shades of green that couldn't be found in the cities no matter what time of year it was. Even when they passed a city, those hills remained in the background, a constant reminder that this trip somehow meant *more.*

He sat at a booth by himself, across the aisle from an older gentleman sipping tea and reading a newspaper. There were several other people in the train car with them, but it was mostly quiet, which Hunter found strange. He figured there would have been people bustling in and out as they awoke, but there was very little through traffic; save for the workers of the train occasionally checking the breakfast buffet to make sure the food was still warm enough.

Toward the end of his meal, as Hunter was getting ready to stand, the older man across from him looked up and called to him.

"Um, lad," he said, with a distinctly Irish accent.

Hunter looked down at him from his now standing position. "Sir, can I help you?"

"I hate to bother you, my boy, but these legs don't work like they used to and I haven't seen one of the train car attendants in quite a spell. I wondered if you wouldn't have it in ya to fill my cup with some fresh tea?"

Hunter nodded, grabbed the man's cup from him and walked to the rear of the train to refill it, returning a moment later with the fresh cup.

"Thank you kindly, my boy." The man took a sip. "Fresh and hot, the way good tea should always be drunk."

Hunter nodded and turned to leave, but the man's voice stopped him again.

"Where are you headed to?"

Hunter thought about it quickly, how silly it sounded to admit he didn't know—but also how freeing it was. But this was a stranger, so what did it matter really?

"I don't know yet. I just know north."

The old man smiled into his cup of tea and took a sip. Hunter turned to leave, figuring that the conversation was over at that point, but just as his back was to the old man, he spoke again.

"Best of luck in finding her, lad," he said.

A chill ran up Hunter's spine, causing him to pause and turn back to his newfound companion.

"I beg your pardon?"

"Well, is it not a girl that motivates your movin'?" the old man asked, chuckling. He didn't even bother to turn and face Hunter as he said it, and Hunter was grateful, for a moment, to be out of his line of sight, protected in his moment of shock from scrutiny.

"I didn't—"

"You need not be saying anything about her for an old man like myself to know it, lad," the man said. "I was once your age, a boy in want of adventure, of love, just the same." His tone took on a far-away wisp to it and his smile grew slightly nostalgic.

Hunter took the half step back into his field of vision. He couldn't contain his curiosity. "Well, did you find it ?"

"Oh, aye. I found everything I was looking for.." The old man looked down into his tea. "When a great purpose like that calls, you answer."

Hunter felt a sense of satisfaction from that. He wished his dad could've heard him say that. *I was called, Dad. I answered.*

Hunter settled back into the booth he'd been in across from the old man and waited. If the man said nothing more, he decided he would be okay with that. But something about this interaction felt important, and he told himself to give it time, to see what would happen..

"Did you . . . did she know you were looking for her?" Hunter asked after several minutes of silence, the curiosity becoming too much for him. He tried to convince himself that it was just curiosity about the man's situation, but he knew that he truly wondered about what would happen between him and Syrena when he showed up at her doorstep.

The man chuckled. "She had no idea who I was. Nearly stabbed me to death with a gardening spade. Told me to leave and never come back."

Hunter's heart sank at that and he was ready to turn away when the man continued speaking.

"But just as I was about to leave, a woman came out of the house. Her mother. She asked me what I was doing there, who I was, and shook my hand. When she saw my ring, this old thing that I'd gotten from my father, she paused. Then she invited me in for tea." The man sighed.

"And what? You got to marry her daughter?" Hunter glanced at the man's hands and saw no ring in sight.

"No, my boy. Sadly, no. See, I wasn't the only one that was looking for the girl. Isn't that the way it always goes? Heroes and quests and love stories, all the things of fairy tales. One thing you need to know about fairy tales, is that they spin them so the hero always gets the girl. There's always a happy ending. But I wasn't the hero in this story. Important, perhaps, but not the hero.

"While we were sitting to tea, there was a knock at the door. Another young man, claiming to need to speak with this woman's daughter. Then a woman came, and another. Four of us in total. All claiming that we had to see this girl, to know her. It wasn't until we were all there that she explained it to us, what we were meant to do, that we were all supposed to be part of this girl's life, to protect her." The man laughed again. "It really was so hard to believe. But even as she told us, none of us refused to leave. I knew the moment that I saw her I wouldn't be able to. That's what love is. It's what love does."

Hunter wondered briefly if that's what he felt for Syrena, if that's why he was doing all of this. Was it even possible to love someone that you had never met?

"Did you end up winning her over like you intended?" Hunter asked, enthralled now with the story.

The old man chuckled and shook his head. "Unfortunately, no. Another young lad there ended up winning her over. There was a lot going on at that time that influenced her decision, but it worked out for the best I suppose. I ended up meetin' the daughter of one of the servants at the mansion, making myself a family and a good life out there in Ireland." The man's eyes turned sad after that. "But she passed just a few years ago now. Plus, there's been stirring up at the old manor house, so I felt it was time I best be moving on."

Hunter's chest ached for the old man, but he pressed on with questions, now needing to know. Now sensing that there was something more to this. Something important that he was missing. "The old manor house?"

"Oh, aye. The woman in my dreams," the old man said, smiling, "was a princess. Sounds silly to say now, but back then we believed in stories, you know. Some of us here in Ireland still do. The myths, legends and lore keep our blood pumping. Some have the fear of God. The rest of us have a fear of magic."

That same chill from before shot through Hunter's body again and he had to suppress a shudder. "You're saying it was magic?"

The old man smiled a knowing smile, but only offered a shrug. "Coincidence works just as well. That manor has held four generations of that woman's family now, and this is the first time that it's been without anyone but the little lady of the place. It leaves a bad feeling in these old bones, and I know when to listen. So I'm headed off to see the places I never got to while I was busy making my living and raising my children."

"You're chasing your adventure," Hunter murmured.

The man winked. "Some things don't change," he confirmed, then swigged the last of his tea before rocking himself onto his feet. "Listen, lad, I know that story seems a touch dreary—me chasing a lass I couldn't get—but I got something better from it and for it. So, whatever it is you're going after, keep going. Even if it's not what you need, what you need will find you."

Hunter nodded and offered the man a smile, then watched as he hobbled slowly out of the meal car and back down to the main seating areas of the train. It wasn't until he was out of sight that Hunter turned back around and settled back into his seat.

For a long time, Hunter was quiet, contemplating all he'd heard from the man. Magic. Coincidences. Chasing a girl he didn't know. And Ireland.

As Hunter recalled it, something chilled in his blood.

Ireland. In his mind, Syrena flashed like a beacon, shining bright and beautiful and pure. *She's in Ireland,* he realized.

Hunter's breathing was faster now, more jagged, as he saw images of a manor house, of a rose garden, and of a woman with raven black hair standing out on a balcony, overlooking rolling green hills.

He knew he had to be on the right path now. The old man was part of all this. He didn't know how, but he knew it. There were coincidences, he decided, but if he was going to chase dreams of a girl and believe all this was real, then he decided that he also needed to believe in magic, just a little bit. So, he threw a silent *thank you* out to the man who'd drank his tea beside him, gathered all his things into his backpack and headed back to his train car.

He knew where he was going now.

I'm coming, Syrena. Somehow. I just hope you know the reason why.

THE TRAIN REACHED THE last station about thirty minutes after the old man left Hunter in the meal car. He wished he could see him one last time, to thank him for what he'd done, even if he wouldn't know why. Now that he knew where she was, he had to get a more direct plan of how to get there.

At the train station, he found a map of the United Kingdom, and looked up a northern port that would ferry him across to Northern Ireland. He silently thanked the universe for making him think of grabbing his passport when he left his house as a "just in case." A quick double check that it was still in his bag, along with the money he needed to purchase his tickets, had him boarding another train that would bring him to Cairnryan, Scotland, where he could hop a ferry to

Ireland. He added the map to his small stash of belongings and settled into the train.

With nothing better to do, his thoughts began to spiral again, the lack of sleep getting to him and not helping his case. He began thinking of Syrena, of how he finally knew where she was, at least generally, and how he was going to make it to her. He thought of the panic of not knowing if he was going to make it to her, about winding up in a city he knew nothing about. Then having to navigate that city, of having to navigate an entirely new country. Would this all work out the way he intended it to? He'd never gone anywhere without his parents before. He had been lucky enough to travel because of his dad due to his position and subsequent income from the foundation. They had been well-off to start because of the inheritance left to them from his grandfather, but his dad worked as hard as anyone and had made substantial wealth of his own in his lifetime. Though he had had the opportunity to travel to many pla throughout the UK and overseas–even to the States—traveling alone for the first time was an entirely different beast. And he was doing it on a whim. His ear grew sore from his constant fiddling with his earring.

When he got hungry, he ate. He still had plenty of granola bars, but still wasn't sure how long he would be on the road. Or, if he would even be able to find her before the curse trapped her in that manor forever on her twenty-first birthday. The only comfort he found came from the ever-present tug he felt from the north.

No, he thought. *Not just the north. Ireland.*

Because he knew where she was now. Even in his attempts to comfort himself, though, the distance was enough to plant deep seeds of doubt within him. By the time he reached his stop, almost as far north as he could get in England, he was about ready to reboard the same train and take it home. Traveling such a long way as his first solo trip was stressful enough, but there was a secondary issue that he couldn't stop mulling over either: what if he didn't make it to her in time? The nagging fear of that time limit still pressed in at the back of his mind, and he hurried to disembark the train despite his best efforts to keep his head on straight. If he had to, he thought he would bite his tongue and call his dad for the money to get him home. *And brag about getting the girl the whole call.* Hunter didn't live to gain his dad's affections anymore, but no one ever fully gave up the desire to prove themselves–and prove those who doubted them wrong in the process–when they could.

There would be smugness in that return, if it ever happened.

The idea that he might not return settled in him like a stone. He was almost grateful for the weight. In a way, it was grounding him. It helped appease some of his anxieties, giving him the chance to relish in the fact that he had made these decisions for himself. Good or bad, he was standing on his own two legs separate from his parents, and that was nothing to sniff at or be ashamed of. If it flopped, it flopped. But he'd stuck to his guns, no matter what, why, or how things turned out. That meant something.

At the train station, he found a map of the train and bus routes, mapped his way down to the ferry yard, and then asked one of the train ticket sellers for a piece of paper and a pen. While he waited for the right bus to pull into the station, he wrote down all that he knew about Syrena and her situation: the way she looked, that she had aged a year in a night, that she lived in a manor. Any detail he could think of, he wrote down.

When the bus pulled into the station, Hunter threw his pen and paper into the backpack and boarded. He counted the number of stops he needed, got a good seat by the window, and settled in for the ride. His next stop would be the ferry, then across the Irish Sea to Ireland, where he was sure Syrena waited for him.

I'm coming, he said to her. *No matter what it takes, I'm coming.*

Chapter Two: Getting To Her

The bus took Hunter directly to the ferry port, for which he was grateful. From there, it was directly from the bus to the ferry ticket window, and then onto the boat.

"You get on here in Cairnryan and it will drop you in Belfast in about three hours," the woman in the ticket box told him as she slid the ticket over.

Hunter thanked her and then made his way toward the line, grateful that for one leg of this journey at least, he wouldn't have to sit and wait for something to progress. No one else had the sense of urgency that he seemed to have regarding his travel, and he was grateful that the ferry was at least *moving* when he was ready to move.

But once he was situated on the ferry, he realized something else: He only knew that Syrena was in Ireland. He had no idea where she was within the country. She could be anywhere. And her time, from what he knew from his dreams, was rapidly running out. If there was anything that he was going to be able to do, he would have to find her, and fast.

The boat embarked shortly after he'd found a seat, and for the three hours that it took for them to cross the water, Hunter tried desperately to sleep, to figure out anything that he could that might get him even a smidge closer to where she was in Ireland, but sleep evaded him. As land grew further behind him and then closer before him, he grew more irate as he realized that the one breakthrough that he had to follow her north was growing cold.

When they arrived in Ireland, Hunter remained seated for as long as he could, lingering until he was one of the last people remaining on the boat, until the security guards were making their rounds and waking the few stragglers that had been lucky enough, in Hunter's eyes, to fall asleep.

As he got off the boat, Hunter looked around, scanning the area for any hints, anything that might look familiar from his dreams or remind him of Syrena, but nothing struck a chord in his memory. He sighed in frustration and shook his head, then made his way from the dock into the main area of Belfast. He had some money left and figured he might as well use some of it to get himself something to eat and listen to the locals to see if maybe they said anything that might help.

He found a pub not far from the docks that looked only slightly run down and had relatively affordable prices judging from the menu posted on the outside of the door. With a deep breath, he stepped inside.

A bell above the door rang, signaling his arrival, and he quickly settled himself at a table by the door. Someone came by with a menu and a glass of water for him, for which he was grateful. He glanced the options over, then settled on a burger and placed his order when the woman returned. It wasn't long before the burger came , as delicious a burger as he had ever had. Pub food, he decided, was always the best food he was going to have.

Outside the window, the sun was starting to go down. It had been a full twenty-four hours since he had left home , and he was still no closer to finding Syrena. He still felt that pull towards her. When he'd reached the ferry port, the pull toward her had shifted slightly, from directly north to the west. He knew that with it getting more accurate , he had to be getting closer, but he still didn't have enough information. He wanted to have an exact location, a town, anything at this point. But he decided that if he couldn't get that, he would still follow his feelings.

Toward the end of his meal, though, when nothing had changed, he decided that perhaps he needed to be a little more proactive with his sleuthing. When the waitress came back to give him her bill, he decided to ask.

"Excuse me. I know this is going to sound most likely incredibly insane, but I was wondering if you knew a woman with dark hair and blue eyes?"

She smiled at him, giggling. "We all know someone who looks like that, love. You got a name?"

Hunter felt somehow that giving out her name was a betrayal, so he just smiled sheepishly and dipped his head. "Sorry to waste your time."

She just shook her head and walked off.

Once he was rung out, Hunter made to leave. He figured through the information he had, tried to decide how much he was willing to give away. If she was really in danger–and he didn't know what kind of danger–would giving her name away put her at risk? Was the risk worth it if it would help him find her? There were so many factors he needed to consider that he couldn't sort through it.

A glance outside told him that the sun was almost down, and he was due for some sleep. He decided that, at the very least, was a safe question to ask someone.

Outside the building, two men were having a beer at one of the sidewalk tables. He approached carefully.

"Excuse me."

One of the men looked up at him. He was gruff, a brown beard shot through with gray, almost brushing against his chest as he assessed Hunter. He must not have seen a threat in him because he tilted his head back.

"Aye?"

A sailor then, Hunter decided.

"Sorry to interrupt you both, but I was hoping you could tell me somewhere I could get a room for the night."

The man smiled and nodded. "There's an inn just two streets down on the left. Good pricing, sweet owner, and best breakfast you'll ever have."

The other man at the table turned and nodded. "Spent a night or two there myself when the missus said the fish smell wouldn't come out of my beard."

Both of the men chuckled at that.

"What are you doing down near the docks, boy? I've not seen you on one of the ships."

Hunter shook his head. "I'm, uh, visiting a friend."

The men gave each other knowing looks before turning back to Hunter.

"You're here for the party, aren't you?" the first man asked.

Hunter's face twisted up in confusion. "The party?"

The second one nodded. "Aye. It's been causing quite a stir up at the manor."

"Four years them doors have been shut, and now, that girl that's all alone, turns twenty and decides to throw a party," the first man continued, shaking his head.

"Is that right? Are you to go?" the second man asked him. The men seemed to have forgotten that Hunter was standing there now, but he refused to move.

A girl in a manor. Syrena?

"The birthday party for a princess with no throne?" The man guffawed. "I have fish to catch and a daughter of my own to feed. There's no party like that in me anymore. Twenty years ago, however . . ."

Hunter stopped listening. He remembered the old man and the mention of the manor. He also knew that Syrena was just turning twenty . Those couldn't be coincidences. At least, it was the only clue he had, so he was going to have to follow it, regardless.

"Sorry, what did you say the name of the manor was?" Hunter asked them, interrupting the reminiscing.

The man with the gray beard turned his attention back to Hunter, seeming confused that he hadn't yet left. "Tara Manor. Up on the hill."

"And there's to be a party?"

"Aye," said the second man. "Tomorrow night, for the princess's birthday."

"Is anyone permitted to attend?" Hunter asked.

The other man at the table snorted, the first sound that Hunter had heard him make.

"*Permitted,*" the stout one echoed. "Aye, boy, she's allowing anyone to attend. It's rumored to be quite the party. Keep your head about you, though; that girl's been locked up for a decade or more."

Hunter's hope grew only a little as he tried to control it. This *had* to be Syrena.

"Thank you, men, for your time."

The men nodded, and Hunter quickly exited from the pub. Tomorrow night, he needed to be at the Tara Manor for that party. In another day, he would be with her. Despite his attempts to not get too excited, he couldn't help but feel slightly giddy at the idea. He was going to find her, be with her. He was going to actually do it.

And if other people were talking about her, Hunter allowed himself to think, *that had to mean that she was real.*

Hunter quickly pulled out the map of Belfast he had scored from the ferry office in Cairnryan and tried his best to navigate the streets to a bus hub, the idea of sleep completely forgotten. When he couldn't use the paper map to find it, he asked more locals who led him in the right direction. Eventually the bus station loomed in front of him, and he let out a relieved breath, the excitement of finally, *finally*, being able to get to her pushing his footsteps a little bit faster.

"Excuse me," he said to the ticket clerk once he was inside. "Excuse me. What is the fastest way to get to Tara from here?"

The man behind the counter gave him a kind smile. "Bus will get you there in a few hours, but the next one doesn't leave until tomorrow."

Hunter's hope fell only a little.

"Are you heading up for the princess' party?" the clerk asked.

Hunter nodded.

The clerk's smile widened a little. "My daughter is going too. We hear it's supposed to be quite the yoke."

Hunter smiled, not exactly sure what a "yoke" was, and asked for a ticket for the earliest bus to Tara, which the clerk gave him. He then found an empty bench within the bus depot, situated his backpack beneath his head, and drifted off to sleep with thoughts of Syrena in his head.

A few hours, Syrena, he cast his thoughts to her. *All that separates us is a few hours. I'm coming.*

Chapter Three: The Party

In the morning, an hour before his bus was supposed to leave, Hunter used the train depot bathroom to clean up as best as he could. With paper towels and hand soap, there wasn't much that he could accomplish, but he did what he could. Then he changed into the other pair of clean pants that he had brought and a clean shirt. When he felt that he was as presentable as he was going to get, he emerged from the bathroom—only to crash directly into someone walking in.

"Woah, hey, watch it," the voice of the other person screamed, distinctly *not* Irish—and not English either. American.

"I'm sorry," Hunter said, reaching down to pick up something he'd knocked free of the other man's hand, only to see that it was a notebook with the picture of a woman doodled on the front of it. His blood ran a little colder–and something sour twisted in his gut–when he recognized the raven black hair and the shape of the eyes, but he tried to smile. "Girlfriend you're missing?"

The other man scowled at him, snatching the notebook away—then seemed to pause when his eyes landed on Hunter's ear, on the earring that hung there. "Just someone I've been lookin' for."

Hunter's blood ran even cooler. He briefly thought again of the man on the train, of the way the man had not been the only one to look for his woman either. It was growing all too similar. "You're a long way from home to be looking for someone." He hated the way his voice tightened, as if in disbelief. But he needed to understand.

The other man eyed him up and down, his brown eyes skeptical behind a curtain of brown curls so dark they were almost black. "What are you gettin' at?"

"The name . . . the woman you're looking for . . ." Hunter hesitated. But this couldn't be a coincidence. He decided to only play some of his cards. "She's important here, a princess. She's having a party tonight at her manor. Lots of people from around here are invited. If you're trying to get close to her—"

"Thanks, pal, but I'm not really goin' to blend in here like some of the other folks. Americans stick out like a sore thumb around here. Best to find another way to her, I think." The man started to walk past him into the bathroom, but Hunter stuck his arm out, gripping his shoulder.

The man didn't turn, but he did angle his head to look at Hunter's fingers over the curve of his shoulder. "I wouldn't do that." Hunter felt the tension in his muscles beneath his shirt sleeve, could see the flex in the other man's bicep beneath the swirls of ink that decorated the skin there. He had more than half a mind to pull his hand away, having never really been a fighter and knowing full well that this guy could probably take him without ever having been in a fight before, but for Syrena's sake, he knew he had to stand his ground.

"Please," Hunter said. "Hear me out."

The man still didn't look at Hunter, but his stance relaxed ever so slightly. He said nothing, as if waiting for Hunter to continue.

So he did. "I'm trying to find her too. I know it sounds crazy, but there's something . . . important . . . that I'm supposed to do with her, I believe. If I can get to her with this party, prove to her that I'm meant to help . . ."

The man was looking at him now, eyes wide with disbelief and maybe a little bit of fear. "You pullin' my chain or somethin'?" the man asked.

Hunter held up his hands in mock surrender and shook his head. "I'm just trying to get to that girl, same as you."

The man sized him up for a long time, head to toe and back again, and then slowly—so painfully slowly—he held out his hand. "Austyn Martin."

Hunter returned the gesture. "I'm Hunter Munroe."

"What do you know about the girl?"

"Only that I have to find her."

Austyn nodded. "Me too."

"Come with me. To the party. Help me look for her."

Austyn shook his head. "Parties are not my territory, man. And with the . . . with all the crazy things that have been coming around surrounding this girl—" he gave Hunter a knowing look, a questioning look, and Hunter nodded. *I've been having dreams too,* he thought, "—all the craziness, I think it best if I just wait until I know exactly where she is, exactly what to expect. What even I'm supposed to say to her. I can't just walk up to a girl—a princess, did you say?—and ask her if she's the Keeper of the White Light that I've been dreaming about for a decade."

Hunter inclined his chin only slightly to acknowledge what Austyn had said, but then his mind remembered up on something that he had said. "Wait, what did you call her?"

"The Keeper of the—wait, are you scammin' me, pal? Did you not—"

"Hey, hey." Hunter held up his hands again. "I just hadn't heard about that part of it is all. That just might not be why *I* need to find her, alright?"

Austyn was a suspicious person, Hunter determined, but the other man nodded.

"I'll go to the party tonight and scope it, okay? Find her. Then if she's the real deal, I'll come back for you. Or meet you somewhere and bring you. Do you have a phone that works over here?"

Austyn shook his head.

Hunter thought for a long moment. "Okay, then you'll have to come on the bus. We can find a place for you to hide out and wait, and I can come get you when it's safe. If it turns out it's not, then we leave back from the estate on the bus together. Is that fair?"

Austyn still didn't seem convinced. "What if you're part of this whole setup?"

"I assure you that I am not making you dream of a girl from another country," Hunter said, his expression incredulous, a statement to which Austyn seemed to cede.

"Alright, I'll come. Let me . . . do my business, and then I'll get the ticket and we can board."

Hunter nodded and let Austyn do what he needed to. While he was alone, Hunter considered what it meant that someone else was dreaming about Syrena. It made sense, in this twisted new reality, that someone else would, especially given what that man on the train had said. He was clear that other people had been involved in it when he was as well. But to have met him like this, to have the entire thing repeat . . . it felt like too much too fast. He couldn't comprehend it.

More than that, there was a small part of him, he had to admit, that didn't like it. For almost a decade, he had been dreaming about this girl. He felt a draw to her, felt her terror and panic, and knew that in some way she needed him. Now to learn that she may also be reaching out to others. He wasn't too prideful to admit that a part of him was jealous. He wanted to be important to her in some way. He thought that, perhaps, there had been more to it than that. It left a bad taste in his mouth, as well as a slight feeling of embarrassment, though he didn't quite know why.

When the other man was ready, tickets in hand, both made their way over to the correct terminal and situated themselves to wait. The closer the bus arrival time came, the more Hunter's stomach twisted into knots. What if he came all this way, chased down a girl, and it wasn't even her? Even with Austyn now sitting at his side, chasing down the same woman, he couldn't be sure this wasn't all entirely made up. What's worse: What if he'd chased her down and he had no idea who she actually was? What if he simply couldn't find her? He was basically stalking this girl at this point. This idea rocked him, nearly sending him away from this bus stop entirely, to a terminal that would take him back to the ferry and across the water home to England.

The idea of home made him scowl, and as the bus rounded the corner, he knew he had to see this through to the end. If not for his sake alone now, then for Austyn's. If there were more people involved at this point than just him, then there had to be more at stake than an overactive imagination. There had to be. Time, money. A train, so many buses, a ferry—he had to know if she would be waiting at the end for him.

Or them, he thought now with a slightly resentful tone in spite of himself. Even if Austyn's involvement helped him to make concrete of the abstract in all of this.

There had to be a reason for the dreams, for that connection he felt, for the fact that another person was also dreaming of her, searching for her. Even his imagination, as active as it was, couldn't conjure up something like this, he was sure of it. There was no way he would be able to make up an entire woman and a slew of people to corroborate her existence—let alone an entire country that believed her to be a princess.

He also counted on the other people on the bus that were dressed to impress and figured that that was consolation enough that at the very least there was an important woman at the end of this journey, and that he was there for a reason. What were the chances that he was coincidentally drawn to this place and dreaming of a woman at the same time that a party for the woman was being held? Slim. Not to mention that at the same time another man would be at the bus station also looking for her.

Reassuring himself in this way got him on the bus and kept him seated for the ride. It helped that Austyn was seated right next to him, sketching away in that notebook of his—pictures of Syrena, pictures of symbols like her heart locket, a rose, a half moon and star—

Hunter paused as he looked at that drawing. It was already sketched, the pencil smudged slightly from the pages rubbing together—an exact depiction of the earring that now hung from his ear.

His hand went up to worry it as he examined the sketch more closely. A vague memory of the other images flashed through his mind, hazy like it had been a dream–because it had.

"Did you just draw that?" Hunter asked, pointing at the depiction of his earring on the page.

Austyn looked at where Hunter had pointed, then up to Hunter's ear, shaking his head slightly. "Two weeks ago . . ." His voice was soft, as if he couldn't quite believe it himself.

Hunter and Austyn shared a knowing look before the latter focused on his sketchbook and Hunter turned back toward the window, a new kind of panic roiling in his gut. It only got worse as they got closer to the manor, as the notion of making a mistake and his dad's voice saying, "I told you so," echoed in his head. But when they rounded that final bend and the manor came into view, it was like every piece of tension in Hunter's body evaporated.

Before them on the hill stood a manor made of bricks and slate, as old as the hill itself seemed to be. It was weathered, but in a way that oozed elegance rather than dilapidation and neglect, with ivy that decorated the bricks on the outside, leaving natural tattoos that paved their way down to sprawling gardens across the estate—the same exact gardens Hunter had seen in his dreams. Those patterns of roses, the colors, were undeniable. He would have been able to recognize them anywhere.

Even from this distance, he could see a flurry of activity as one of the servants of the manor prepared the grounds for the coming party. It wasn't for several hours yet, set to start just before sunset—Syrena's favorite time of day, when the garden was the prettiest, as he knew from the dreams. The preparations seemed to have already been in the works for hours now. He could also see movement from within the manor, as the curtains were dusted and the people from within flurried back and forth behind the windows. He thought it actually looked quite funny, and out of context with no sound.

The bus slowed at the base of the hill that the manor resided atop, and a butler dressed in a perfectly fitted and pressed black suit greeted them as soon as they exited.

"Good day, everyone," he said loudly. "I am sure that you are all excited to approach the manor and greet Princess Syrena for her special day."

Austyn tensed beside him, and he realized that Austyn hadn't known her name. That had been Hunter's secret up until this point. For some reason, he reveled in it.

"However," the butler continued, "there is still much to prepare within and outside of the manor in order for her to feel as though the house is ready to receive so many guests, so please, if you'll follow me. There will be a complimentary tour of the grounds as well as a tea and snack tray mid-afternoon. Once the house is prepared for the party, you will also be allowed to tour there. When the party commences tonight, it is *then* that you will be able to interact with the lady. So please, everyone, this way, this way."

Austyn and Hunter shared a glance and hung back so that they would be the last ones in the group. When they were a safe distance from the others to not look like stragglers but also not be overheard, Hunter spoke.

"While the tour is ongoing, we can find a place for you to hide. That way if I am able to get to the princess, I can come find you and either bring her to you or bring you to her."

Austyn nodded, and the two of them rejoined the group.

The butler led them away from the house to the left and everyone followed, though their heads craned for a glimpse of the mysterious lady of the manor, locked away for a decade, only to throw the doors open on the birthday following the passing of her father. Even Hunter had to admit that he was craning his neck, hoping for a glimpse of her, anything to confirm that this was not just the house but also the girl—the woman—that he had been dreaming of.

Unfortunately, he didn't see her. All through the tour of the grounds, the gardens, during tea, and even during the tour inside the house—during which Austyn very subtly and expertly disappeared into one of the guest rooms in the guest wing—Syrena stayed hidden away. Not one single glimpse of her was seen by a single person of the party, and some people who were there simply to get a glimpse of that which no one had seen in a long time—including the house and the people within it—were gravely disappointed. But Hunter was more than excited. The air of mystery surrounding all of it only made him feel more like he was in the right place and doing the right thing.

By the time the sun had started to set and people were herded back towards the main gardens near the house, Hunter's nerves started up again, this time mixed with excitement. This was it. This would be the moment of truth. Whatever it was that he needed to do for her, this was going to be the catalyst.

To ensure the princess' safety, as they entered the garden, a butler took everyone's name down. Hunter got into line with everyone else and waited patiently while the others gave their information.

He scanned the side of the house as they moved forward, and could have sworn that he saw a curtain move in one of the windows—the window in the room that Austyn had slipped into. He looked around quickly, hoping that no one else saw, and sent a silent thought to Austyn to keep quiet and hidden.

It was his turn now in the line. As he approached, the butler looked him up and down. "Name."

"Hunter Munroe."

The man began to write it down as a woman came over to him in a flurry. She was not dressed like a servant, but in refined clothing that placed her below the nobles but above the common folk. A woman in a class of her own. "I have to take over for you. They need someone to—"

The woman seemed to catch sight of Hunter at that moment and stopped dead in her tracks. She took in his blond hair, his eyes—gray as storm clouds—his earring, and the way he wore only jeans and a t-shirt.

"Oh, that's not going to do." She turned back to the butler. "Forget what I was just saying. I need you to take this boy and get him into nicer clothes as soon as possible. Before the princess sees him."

"Mrs. Scott?" The butler looked baffled. Hunter couldn't blame him. He was pretty taken aback as well.

"Look at his eyes," Mrs. Scott said.

The butler turned to Hunter and did as he was asked. As he looked, the butler's eyebrows nearly went to his hairline. He turned back to the woman and said, "Right away, Miss, right away." He turned to Hunter. "Follow me, boy. Hunter, was it? Quickly, now. Quickly."

Hunter's confusion only mounted, but he followed the butler as he led him toward the manor, then down a hallway to one of the bedrooms. He vaguely recognized it from the tour.

"Inside, inside. Before Lady Syrena sees you. We can't have her seeing you in these clothes now."

"Sir, I beg, what is happening?"

"That's none of your concern right now, and none of my story to tell. In this wardrobe is a stash of clothes for the men that live here when we're out of our working attire. Some of it should fit. Change quickly and then knock on the door so that I may lead you back down to the party." He shut the door before Hunter could ask any further questions, which mounted even as he did as he was told.

He quickly picked out a pair of black slacks and a blue button up shirt that was just slightly too big but closer to fitting his size than anything else in the closet. As a last second decision, he ditched his sneakers for a pair of polished shoes from the bottom of the wardrobe. When he was satisfied with the way the clothes fell, he slung his bag back over his shoulder, his clothes secured inside and knocked on the door.

The butler opened it, gave him a once over, and nodded. "Give me that sack. I'll stash it. You just find me when you'll be needing it back. Follow me, I'll bring you down the back way out to the garden. Hurry now, boy."

Hunter followed the butler back out to the gardens, already bathed in the light of the setting sun. The butler made sure he was outside, mingled in with the crowd, and then disappeared. Without his clothes or his pack, Hunter felt naked, exposed. But he remembered his mission—that he was here for Syrena. And now Austyn, too. He searched within himself, found that tug, and followed it as best he could through the dancing people, towards where he hoped she would be waiting.

HUNTER DECIDED THAT a party was a terrible place to try to find someone that you had never met. Even knowing what she looked like, when you were trying to find someone that didn't know you were looking for them, they didn't know to stay still. Whenever he thought he was finally getting close enough to catch her through their bond, the bond would lengthen, signaling that she had moved.

It went on like that for hours, with him getting closer to her and then her moving away. He tried his best to act casually, interacting with the guests whenever he crossed paths with them, starting small talk whenever it seemed appropriate. He learned that he was not the only person that was from out of the country that had come to the party. Reminders like that had him glancing up to the window to where Austyn was stashed—but he tried to keep the glances to a minimum, worried about giving his new-found partner-in-crime away.

He also learned that, as with his tour group from earlier, many people had come because of the historical significance of the house, but there were others that had come to witness the mysterious girl that had been locked up inside. It was an interesting thing to witness and be a part of, he decided.

At some point after dark, Hunter decided to take a break and receded towards the bar back near the entrance to the gardens. He ordered a gin and tonic, then turned to face toward the crowd, assessing it. She was close, that much was clear from how tight the bond now felt within him, but where she was, he couldn't be sure.

Then, out of the corner of his eye, he caught movement. A flash of white, a twirl of black, as a group of men off to his right laughed heartily. There she was, floating through the crowd as if in slow motion, arms raised, feet moving in time to the music, blue sapphire eyes meeting his storm cloud gray ones, as his breath caught in his chest.

Syrena.

Chapter Three: The Party

In the morning, an hour before his bus was supposed to leave, Hunter used the train depot bathroom to clean up as best as he could. With paper towels and hand soap, there wasn't much that he could accomplish, but he did what he could. Then he changed into the other pair of clean pants that he had brought and a clean shirt. When he felt that he was as presentable as he was going to get, he emerged from the bathroom—only to crash directly into someone walking in.

"Woah, hey, watch it," the voice of the other person screamed, distinctly *not* Irish—and not English either. American.

"I'm sorry," Hunter said, reaching down to pick up something he'd knocked free of the other man's hand, only to see that it was a notebook with the picture of a woman doodled on the front of it. His blood ran a little colder–and something sour twisted in his gut–when he recognized the raven black hair and the shape of the eyes, but he tried to smile. "Girlfriend you're missing?"

The other man scowled at him, snatching the notebook away—then seemed to pause when his eyes landed on Hunter's ear, on the earring that hung there. "Just someone I've been lookin' for."

Hunter's blood ran even cooler. He briefly thought again of the man on the train, of the way the man had not been the only one to look for his woman either. It was growing all too similar. "You're a long way from home to be looking for someone." He hated the way his voice tightened, as if in disbelief. But he needed to understand.

The other man eyed him up and down, his brown eyes skeptical behind a curtain of brown curls so dark they were almost black. "What are you gettin' at?"

"The name . . . the woman you're looking for . . ." Hunter hesitated. But this couldn't be a coincidence. He decided to only play some of his cards. "She's important here, a princess. She's having a party tonight at her manor. Lots of people from around here are invited. If you're trying to get close to her—"

"Thanks, pal, but I'm not really goin' to blend in here like some of the other folks. Americans stick out like a sore thumb around here. Best to find another way to her, I think." The man started to walk past him into the bathroom, but Hunter stuck his arm out, gripping his shoulder.

The man didn't turn, but he did angle his head to look at Hunter's fingers over the curve of his shoulder. "I wouldn't do that." Hunter felt the tension in his muscles beneath his shirt sleeve, could see the flex in the other man's bicep beneath the swirls of ink that decorated the skin there. He had more than half a mind to pull his hand away, having never really been a fighter and knowing full well that this guy could probably take him without ever having been in a fight before, but for Syrena's sake, he knew he had to stand his ground.

"Please," Hunter said. "Hear me out."

The man still didn't look at Hunter, but his stance relaxed ever so slightly. He said nothing, as if waiting for Hunter to continue.

So he did. "I'm trying to find her too. I know it sounds crazy, but there's something . . . important . . . that I'm supposed to do with her, I believe. If I can get to her with this party, prove to her that I'm meant to help . . ."

The man was looking at him now, eyes wide with disbelief and maybe a little bit of fear. "You pullin' my chain or somethin'?" the man asked.

Hunter held up his hands in mock surrender and shook his head. "I'm just trying to get to that girl, same as you."

The man sized him up for a long time, head to toe and back again, and then slowly—so painfully slowly—he held out his hand. "Austyn Martin."

Hunter returned the gesture. "I'm Hunter Munroe."

"What do you know about the girl?"

"Only that I have to find her."

Austyn nodded. "Me too."

"Come with me. To the party. Help me look for her."

Austyn shook his head. "Parties are not my territory, man. And with the . . . with all the crazy things that have been coming around surrounding this girl—" he gave Hunter a knowing look, a questioning look, and Hunter nodded. *I've been having dreams too,* he thought, "—all the craziness, I think it best if I just wait until I know exactly where she is, exactly what to expect. What even I'm supposed to say to her. I can't just walk up to a girl—a princess, did you say?—and ask her if she's the Keeper of the White Light that I've been dreaming about for a decade."

Hunter inclined his chin only slightly to acknowledge what Austyn had said, but then his mind remembered up on something that he had said. "Wait, what did you call her?"

"The Keeper of the—wait, are you scammin' me, pal? Did you not—"

"Hey, hey." Hunter held up his hands again. "I just hadn't heard about that part of it is all. That just might not be why *I* need to find her, alright?"

Austyn was a suspicious person, Hunter determined, but the other man nodded.

"I'll go to the party tonight and scope it, okay? Find her. Then if she's the real deal, I'll come back for you. Or meet you somewhere and bring you. Do you have a phone that works over here?"

Austyn shook his head.

Hunter thought for a long moment. "Okay, then you'll have to come on the bus. We can find a place for you to hide out and wait, and I can come get you when it's safe. If it turns out it's not, then we leave back from the estate on the bus together. Is that fair?"

Austyn still didn't seem convinced. "What if you're part of this whole setup?"

"I assure you that I am not making you dream of a girl from another country," Hunter said, his expression incredulous, a statement to which Austyn seemed to cede.

"Alright, I'll come. Let me . . . do my business, and then I'll get the ticket and we can board."

Hunter nodded and let Austyn do what he needed to. While he was alone, Hunter considered what it meant that someone else was dreaming about Syrena. It made sense, in this twisted new reality, that someone else would, especially given what that man on the train had said. He was clear that other people had been involved in it when he was as well. But to have met him like this, to have the entire thing repeat . . . it felt like too much too fast. He couldn't comprehend it.

More than that, there was a small part of him, he had to admit, that didn't like it. For almost a decade, he had been dreaming about this girl. He felt a draw to her, felt her terror and panic, and knew that in some way she needed him. Now to learn that she may also be reaching out to others. He wasn't too prideful to admit that a part of him was jealous. He wanted to be important to her in some way. He thought that, perhaps, there had been more to it than that. It left a bad taste in his mouth, as well as a slight feeling of embarrassment, though he didn't quite know why.

When the other man was ready, tickets in hand, both made their way over to the correct terminal and situated themselves to wait. The closer the bus arrival time came, the more Hunter's stomach twisted into knots. What if he came all this way, chased down a girl, and it wasn't even her? Even with Austyn now sitting at his side, chasing down the same woman, he couldn't be sure this wasn't all entirely made up. What's worse: What if he'd chased her down and he had no idea who she actually was? What if he simply couldn't find her? He was basically stalking this girl at this point. This idea rocked him, nearly sending him away from this bus stop entirely, to a terminal that would take him back to the ferry and across the water home to England.

The idea of home made him scowl, and as the bus rounded the corner, he knew he had to see this through to the end. If not for his sake alone now, then for Austyn's. If there were more people involved at this point than just him, then there had to be more at stake than an overactive imagination. There had to be. Time, money. A train, so many buses, a ferry—he had to know if she would be waiting at the end for him.

Or them, he thought now with a slightly resentful tone in spite of himself. Even if Austyn's involvement helped him to make concrete of the abstract in all of this.

There had to be a reason for the dreams, for that connection he felt, for the fact that another person was also dreaming of her, searching for her. Even his imagination, as active as it was, couldn't conjure up something like this, he was sure of it. There was no way he would be able to make up an entire woman and a slew of people to corroborate her existence—let alone an entire country that believed her to be a princess.

He also counted on the other people on the bus that were dressed to impress and figured that that was consolation enough that at the very least there was an important woman at the end of this journey, and that he was there for a reason. What were the chances that he was coincidentally drawn to this place and dreaming of a woman at the same time that a party for the woman was being held? Slim. Not to mention that at the same time another man would be at the bus station also looking for her.

Reassuring himself in this way got him on the bus and kept him seated for the ride. It helped that Austyn was seated right next to him, sketching away in that notebook of his—pictures of Syrena, pictures of symbols like her heart locket, a rose, a half moon and star—

Hunter paused as he looked at that drawing. It was already sketched, the pencil smudged slightly from the pages rubbing together—an exact depiction of the earring that now hung from his ear. His hand went up to worry it as he examined the sketch more closely. A vague memory of the other images flashed through his mind, hazy like it had been a dream–because it had.

"Did you just draw that?" Hunter asked, pointing at the depiction of his earring on the page.

Austyn looked at where Hunter had pointed, then up to Hunter's ear, shaking his head slightly. "Two weeks ago . . ." His voice was soft, as if he couldn't quite believe it himself.

Hunter and Austyn shared a knowing look before the latter focused on his sketchbook and Hunter turned back toward the window, a new kind of panic roiling in his gut. It only got worse as they got closer to the manor, as the notion of making a mistake and his dad's voice saying, "I told you so," echoed in his head. But when they rounded that final bend and the manor came into view, it was like every piece of tension in Hunter's body evaporated.

Before them on the hill stood a manor made of bricks and slate, as old as the hill itself seemed to be. It was weathered, but in a way that oozed elegance rather than dilapidation and neglect, with ivy that decorated the bricks on the outside, leaving natural tattoos that paved their way down to sprawling gardens across the estate—the same exact gardens Hunter had seen in his dreams. Those patterns of roses, the colors, were undeniable. He would have been able to recognize them anywhere.

Even from this distance, he could see a flurry of activity as one of the servants of the manor prepared the grounds for the coming party. It wasn't for several hours yet, set to start just before sunset—Syrena's favorite time of day, when the garden was the prettiest, as he knew from the dreams. The preparations seemed to have already been in the works for hours now. He could also see movement from within the manor, as the curtains were dusted and the people from within flurried back and forth behind the windows. He thought it actually looked quite funny, and out of context with no sound.

The bus slowed at the base of the hill that the manor resided atop, and a butler dressed in a perfectly fitted and pressed black suit greeted them as soon as they exited.

"Good day, everyone," he said loudly. "I am sure that you are all excited to approach the manor and greet Princess Syrena for her special day."

Austyn tensed beside him, and he realized that Austyn hadn't known her name. That had been Hunter's secret up until this point. For some reason, he reveled in it.

"However," the butler continued, "there is still much to prepare within and outside of the manor in order for her to feel as though the house is ready to receive so many guests, so please, if you'll follow me. There will be a complimentary tour of the grounds as well as a tea and snack tray mid-afternoon. Once the house is prepared for the party, you will also be allowed to tour there. When the party commences tonight, it is *then* that you will be able to interact with the lady. So please, everyone, this way, this way."

Austyn and Hunter shared a glance and hung back so that they would be the last ones in the group. When they were a safe distance from the others to not look like stragglers but also not be overheard, Hunter spoke.

"While the tour is ongoing, we can find a place for you to hide. That way if I am able to get to the princess, I can come find you and either bring her to you or bring you to her."

Austyn nodded, and the two of them rejoined the group.

The butler led them away from the house to the left and everyone followed, though their heads craned for a glimpse of the mysterious lady of the manor, locked away for a decade, only to throw the doors open on the birthday following the passing of her father. Even Hunter had to admit that he was craning his neck, hoping for a glimpse of her, anything to confirm that this was not just the house but also the girl—the woman—that he had been dreaming of.

Unfortunately, he didn't see her. All through the tour of the grounds, the gardens, during tea, and even during the tour inside the house—during which Austyn very subtly and expertly disappeared into one of the guest rooms in the guest wing—Syrena stayed hidden away. Not one single glimpse of her was seen by a single person of the party, and some people who were there simply to get a glimpse of that which no one had seen in a long time—including the house and the people within it—were gravely disappointed. But Hunter was more than excited. The air of mystery surrounding all of it only made him feel more like he was in the right place and doing the right thing.

By the time the sun had started to set and people were herded back towards the main gardens near the house, Hunter's nerves started up again, this time mixed with excitement. This was it. This would be the moment of truth. Whatever it was that he needed to do for her, this was going to be the catalyst.

To ensure the princess' safety, as they entered the garden, a butler took everyone's name down. Hunter got into line with everyone else and waited patiently while the others gave their information.

He scanned the side of the house as they moved forward, and could have sworn that he saw a curtain move in one of the windows—the window in the room that Austyn had slipped into. He looked around quickly, hoping that no one else saw, and sent a silent thought to Austyn to keep quiet and hidden.

It was his turn now in the line. As he approached, the butler looked him up and down. "Name."

"Hunter Munroe."

The man began to write it down as a woman came over to him in a flurry. She was not dressed like a servant, but in refined clothing that placed her below the nobles but above the common folk. A woman in a class of her own. "I have to take over for you. They need someone to—"

The woman seemed to catch sight of Hunter at that moment and stopped dead in her tracks. She took in his blond hair, his eyes—gray as storm clouds—his earring, and the way he wore only jeans and a t-shirt.

"Oh, that's not going to do." She turned back to the butler. "Forget what I was just saying. I need you to take this boy and get him into nicer clothes as soon as possible. Before the princess sees him."

"Mrs. Scott?" The butler looked baffled. Hunter couldn't blame him. He was pretty taken aback as well.

"Look at his eyes," Mrs. Scott said.

The butler turned to Hunter and did as he was asked. As he looked, the butler's eyebrows nearly went to his hairline. He turned back to the woman and said, "Right away, Miss, right away." He turned to Hunter. "Follow me, boy. Hunter, was it? Quickly, now. Quickly."

Hunter's confusion only mounted, but he followed the butler as he led him toward the manor, then down a hallway to one of the bedrooms. He vaguely recognized it from the tour.

"Inside, inside. Before Lady Syrena sees you. We can't have her seeing you in these clothes now."

"Sir, I beg, what is happening?"

"That's none of your concern right now, and none of my story to tell. In this wardrobe is a stash of clothes for the men that live here when we're out of our working attire. Some of it should fit. Change quickly and then knock on the door so that I may lead you back down to the party." He shut the door before Hunter could ask any further questions, which mounted even as he did as he was told.

He quickly picked out a pair of black slacks and a blue button up shirt that was just slightly too big but closer to fitting his size than anything else in the closet. As a last second decision, he ditched his sneakers for a pair of polished shoes from the bottom of the wardrobe. When he was satisfied with the way the clothes fell, he slung his bag back over his shoulder, his clothes secured inside and knocked on the door.

The butler opened it, gave him a once over, and nodded. "Give me that sack. I'll stash it. You just find me when you'll be needing it back. Follow me, I'll bring you down the back way out to the garden. Hurry now, boy."

Hunter followed the butler back out to the gardens, already bathed in the light of the setting sun. The butler made sure he was outside, mingled in with the crowd, and then disappeared. Without his clothes or his pack, Hunter felt naked, exposed. But he remembered his mission—that he was here for Syrena. And now Austyn, too. He searched within himself, found that tug, and followed it as best he could through the dancing people, towards where he hoped she would be waiting.

HUNTER DECIDED THAT a party was a terrible place to try to find someone that you had never met. Even knowing what she looked like, when you were trying to find someone that didn't know you were looking for them, they didn't know to stay still. Whenever he thought he was finally getting close enough to catch her through their bond, the bond would lengthen, signaling that she had moved.

It went on like that for hours, with him getting closer to her and then her moving away. He tried his best to act casually, interacting with the guests whenever he crossed paths with them, starting small talk whenever it seemed appropriate. He learned that he was not the only person that was from out of the country that had come to the party. Reminders like that had him glancing up to the window to where Austyn was stashed—but he tried to keep the glances to a minimum, worried about giving his new-found partner-in-crime away.

He also learned that, as with his tour group from earlier, many people had come because of the historical significance of the house, but there were others that had come to witness the mysterious girl that had been locked up inside. It was an interesting thing to witness and be a part of, he decided.

At some point after dark, Hunter decided to take a break and receded towards the bar back near the entrance to the gardens. He ordered a gin and tonic, then turned to face toward the crowd, assessing it. She was close, that much was clear from how tight the bond now felt within him, but where she was, he couldn't be sure.

Then, out of the corner of his eye, he caught movement. A flash of white, a twirl of black, as a group of men off to his right laughed heartily. There she was, floating through the crowd as if in slow motion, arms raised, feet moving in time to the music, blue sapphire eyes meeting his storm cloud gray ones, as his breath caught in his chest.

Syrena.

Chapter Four: The Build-Up

It took a year for them to gather everyone that they needed to break the curse. Through it all, Hunter remained at Syrena's side–being her support when she needed it, her friend when she had no one, and her comfort when she felt weak. The curse took a lot from her, and continued to do so. Without her parents, she felt alone, and he wanted more than anything to remind her that she wasn't.

In the beginning, it was just the three of them–her, Hunter, and Austyn–living in the manor with the people who worked there as they tried to decipher what it was that they needed to do. The glowing woman–who he'd learned was named Luna–had given them even less to go on than he'd thought. His dreams had only given him glimpses, but those glimpses seemed to be about as much information as they had to go off of anyway so it didn't matter.

Slowly, though, things started to come together.

On a rainy night at the manor, a girl named Jupiter came to the door–and that was how the second sign came to them with a rose necklace clasped around her neck. With her arrival in the manor, the atmosphere shifted. There was new vigor in their search for answers and understanding. They started asking more questions, discussing their dreams, and–more than that–understanding each other.

For the first time in a very long time, Hunter felt like he was part of something. He had friends, a family even, that wanted and needed him and that he wanted and needed in return. It became bigger than just breaking the curse. It was finding all of them within this.

That sense of belonging didn't detract from the fact that Syrena's twenty-first was still closing in on them, though, and the curse's timeline with it. They still had someone to find, and they didn't know how to even go about finding him.

Austyn was aggressive in his suggestions, offering to bang on every door in Tara until someone showed up, but Hunter argued against that by making the point that all three of them–Austyn, Hunter, and Jupiter–had come from outside of Tara. Jupiter had come from Paris, Austyn from New Jersey in the States, and Hunter from Essex. Austyn had grumbled but ceded the point. He was nothing if not stubborn and cranky about everything.

It was a chance encounter that finally brought them Phoenix, a skater kid with a sun ring passed down from a father he no longer spoke to. Their stories, all eerily similar, is what brought them close and kept them bonded when the curse finally timed out and they were forced to break it.

Standing in the foyer of the manor, eyes locked, they all shared a nod, and a look, and began.

PART TWO: THE AFTER

Chapter Five: Breaking the Curse

An overpowering gust of air slammed all of them backward, sending Hunter into the wall behind him, then radiating sharp pains through his right hip and shoulder blade, where he connected with the wall. A wave of dizziness went through his head and it took him several seconds to find his limbs and push himself back to his feet, groaning as he did so.

He looked around, trying to make sure that everyone was okay, and saw the other three that had helped them break the curse—Austyn, Jupiter, and Phoenix—scattered about the room in various states of injury and disarray. They had spent the last year searching for the various signs–each possessing a different charm that was needed to help break Syrenas curse. Hunter and Austyn hadn't known at the time, but they'd both been seeing them right along: a rose for Jupiter's necklace, a cross for Austyn's own bracelet, and a sun for Phoenix's ring. Nyx had been the hardest one to track down, and they'd come in just under the wire. They'd done it though. They were all here, all breaking the curse. All for her.

Then he saw Syrena. In the center of the room, her body was suspended in the air, surrounded by a golden light—the same golden light that had emanated from them as they tried to break the curse. Her eyes were closed tightly as she hovered, appearing almost too still. Panic grabbed at Hunter's throat as he forced his feet toward her. The growing discomfort of his panic was matched with a growing pressure in his right ear as he got closer to Syrena's glowing body.

The pressure continued to build until it got to be too much for him, and he was forced to take a step back. The others also got to their feet, looking up at Syrena.

"Is she okay?" Phoenix asked.

"I don't know," Hunter said, shrugging. Inside he was still a panicked mess. "She's not moving."

"We have to do something," Austyn said, staring up at her with the same level of worry in his eyes that Hunter felt. "We can't just leave her like this."

Hunter tried to respond, but the pain in his ear came back, throbbing and hot, and he couldn't do anything but clutch at it.

"Hey, your ear!"

Hunter looked over at Jupiter, whose eyes were locked on his ear as she approached. Another shock of pain had him squeezing his eyes shut again.

"It's glowing," the little girl said.

Hunter tried to look for the light despite it being attached to him, then realized what he was doing and scowled at himself, hoping no one else had seen what he was trying to do. He moved his hand away a bit. "What do you mean, 'it's glowing'?"

"She's right," Austyn said, also coming closer. "Wait." He narrowed his eyes and leaned in. Hunter tried to stay as still as possible, even as the pain continued to build. "It's not your ear; it's your earring!"

"My earring?" Hunter's fingertips moved to the piece of jewelry almost unconsciously. It had been a habit to worry it since he got it, but it was just a piece of jewelry. He hadn't been part of all of this—just had been part of bringing them all together. Hadn't he?

"The sun and moon earring." Jupiter looked at him. "Are you a sign?"

Hunter's eyes bounced between the two of them, confusion swirling within him. He had no idea what they were talking about. All his life, he'd never heard anything about signs. Even when this whole thing had started, when he sent himself off to look for Syrena months before, he hadn't known anything about the White Light, what the signs were, what it meant for her to be a keeper. *Was it possible that he actually was one of them, and no one had ever known it?* His dad had given him that earring when they went to get the piercing on his eighteenth birthday. All he had been told about it was that it was a family heirloom. His mother had given it to him and explained that it was important that he have it. When he'd pushed her about why, she said she didn't know, only that his grandfather insisted he have it, but that his father had refused to pass it along, so she'd agreed to do it for him. She didn't know any more than that.

He tried to picture his dad being one of the signs, being a mystical keeper of a sign for a princess meant to break her curse. The image wouldn't come. His dad—an academic who wanted nothing but the same for his son—was not a sign. He wouldn't ever have been found in a circle like this. Even being part of it now, seeing it with his own eyes, he doubted his dad would believe him when he returned home.

"Is anyone else's charm glowing?" Austyn asked, drawing Hunter's attention back. He could worry about his dad and family lineage later. Right now, the only person he should focus on is Syrena.

Everyone looked at their charms–Jupiter to her necklace, Austyn to his bracelet, and Nyx to his ring–to find that all of them lay dormant, back to normal since the breaking of the curse.

"It's just yours." Phoenix nodded his head at Hunter.

Hunter looked at Syrena's glowing body, still suspended in the middle of the room. *It was not just his charm,* he thought to himself.

"It has to mean something," Jupiter said, seeming to follow his gaze. "You have to mean something."

Hunter turned his gaze away from Syrena to look at Jupiter and Austyn. "Each time I step towards her, my ear hurts."

"You have to try." Austyn took him by the shoulders and made eye contact with him. "She needs you."

Hunter looked at Syrena again, determination building within him, then nodded and started moving toward her. The closer he got, the more his ear started to throb, until it became nearly unbearable again. When it was almost to the point where he felt he needed to step back, he took the earring off and held it in his hand. It was then that he realized that vibrations were coming from the stud itself. He continued forward, the vibrations growing more violent as he drew nearer to Syrena. Hunter gritted his teeth against the pain but kept going. A low hum sounded when he was only a few feet from her, rising in pitch the closer he got to her but he pushed on until he reached her.

Syrena was completely motionless, with not even a flitter of her eyelids to let him know she knew that he was there. His mind was a mess, thoughts running in every direction as he tried to think of what he was supposed to do next. The others had taken their signs and put them together to break the curse, but he was out on his own. He knew she was still in there somewhere though. Despite the stillness of her body, the lifeless way she appeared , he could feel the bond between them, still tugging him towards her. Through it all, he had been able to feel it.

Looking at her like that, he remembered talking to her that first night at the manor—how she had blushed as they talked. He also realized that he had started falling for her. How he felt about her was no easy thing to let go at this point. It had nothing to do with their bond or that she was a princess, someone with position, or even that they had been part of this keeper quest for the last year. It had everything to do with who Syrena was as a person. The way she carried herself, her compassion, the way she went about her life despite everything that had been thrown at her. There was no arrogance—only love and kindness for others. He realized then that there was a place for him in this world, finally. There was no place for him back in England, but here, by her side, he had never known more about himself.

With surprising clarity, what he had to do next came to him. He took a step closer to her. The golden glow that encompassed her was warm to the touch, almost as warm as she was as he wrapped his arm around her waist and pulled her to him. Suspended in the air like this, it was as if she were completely weightless, weighing less than the air itself. As he pulled her to him, the weightlessness left her, until he was holding her. He bent at the knees, cradling her softly in his lap as he wrapped her tightly to his chest.

"Syrena," he said softly. Anxiety coursed through his veins at her silence. Only the bond and the warmth of her body calmed him. She couldn't be dead. "I don't know if you can hear me. If you can, I want you to know that I don't want to come visit every now and again, like I said. I don't want to because I want to stay here with you. If you'll have me."

Still, she didn't stir. The arm that was wrapped around her waist held the still vibrating earring. With the other free hand, he stroked her hair, begging her silently to wake up. He didn't know what else to do.

Desperate, he glanced at the others, then back at her. His eyes searched her face, then landed on her lips, which sparked an idea. *This has been like a fairytale the whole time. What if it has to end like one too?*

With a deep breath, he slowly leaned up and pressed his lips to hers. Warmth enveloped him as he kissed her, even as a breeze swirled around them. He could barely focus on his lips being on hers, no less wonder where the wind came from. He held the kiss for only a few seconds before pulling away.

As soon as their lips separated, the warmth left him. Eyes open again, he scanned her face for any changes, but there were none. She still glowed, but there was no movement beneath her eyelids, no response in her features. Still, even like this, she was the most beautiful woman that he had ever seen.

He continued to beg silently for her to wake, but still no response came. He started to wrack his brain for other ways that he might wake her, then suddenly, he felt a gentle squeeze of his hands. His eyes focused on her face , just in time to see her eyelids opening and her sapphire blue irises meet his . A smile spread across her lips as her free hand came up to caress the side of his face.

"I will have you," she said softly.

Hunter's heart filled with joy as he pulled her into another kiss, relief flooding him. He held her tightly, as if he wasn't ever going to let her go.

Chapter Six: The Keeper of the White Light

"Alright, we get it already!" Austyn called from behind them after a long moment. But there was relief in his voice too, Hunter noted, even as he pulled away from Syrena.

Everyone was staring at them, though Jupiter was the only one that appeared happy. She was positively beaming.

"It's about time," the little girl exclaimed. "Austyn and I were wondering when you two would just admit it."

"You were wondering," Austyn corrected. "I told you it was just a matter of time."

Hunter turned back to Syrena, too overcome with relief in knowing she was okay to press them about any potential conversations they had held over their romantic encounters. He hadn't thought he'd been obvious about his feelings—especially since he hadn't even known about them until she lay unconscious in his arms. Up until that point, she had just been a woman he knew he needed to help. But now . . . now he couldn't picture doing anything without her by his side.

"So, does this mean we did it?" Phoenix asked. "You're okay? The curse is gone?"

Syrena pushed away from Hunter gently and got to her feet. Hunter watched her closely, making sure that she did not wobble, that she was steady and unharmed from the blast that had sent them all flying. In the aftermath of the excitement, with his adrenaline wearing off, Hunter's shoulder and hip were starting to demand his attention again, but he refused to give it. Instead he kept his eyes on the woman before him—no longer glowing and looking for everything that had transpired, okay.

"I don't feel any different," she said. She looked toward Hunter, who had now gotten to his feet and was standing close by in case she needed him. "I don't know."

There was a sudden flash of light, and everyone raised their hands to block their eyes as they each shouted in alarm. Hunter stepped between the light and Syrena, determined to keep it from touching her. She had been through enough. They all had, really. But the light faded after only a second, and a woman stood in the corner of the room who hadn't been there a moment before.

Hunter recognized her from one of his dreams, one of the ones that Syrena had discussed the curse in. He couldn't recall her saying a name, but he immediately got a bad feeling about her. Though he turned to see where the woman was, watching her, he did not remove himself from the path between her and Syrena. She would have to go through him first to get to her.

Hunter noted the smile on the woman's face, however, and realized that it was not one of malice or a place of anger.

"You have done well, child," she said, approaching them. "The curse has been broken."

The group cheered around them, Hunter turning to Syrena to see her beaming at the news as she took in her celebrating friends. She reached out, her smile turning full force on him as she took his hand. He entwined their fingers, barely able to breathe at the sensation of it, at the sight of her joy.

"The town is safe from the Dark Keepers and the curse?" Syrena asked, turning back to the glowing woman.

The woman was nodding. "Because of you, yes."

"It wasn't just me." Syrena gestured at the group of friends with her hand. "I had a lot of help. Even from you, Luna. Thank you for bringing the signs to me."

Luna paused a few steps away from the couple, her smile fading ever so slightly. "I did not bring them, Syrena. Your purity and gentle heart drew the four signs to you."

"But I didn't even know there *were* four signs," Syrena said, raising her and Hunter's conjoined hands. "I never even saw Hunter's earring as one of the charms."

Hunter was ready to jump in and defend her. They had all seen his charm; it was just that none of them had known what to look for. Even he, who had carried it on his body for years, had received it as a gift, hadn't known the significance of it. Anger welled in him ever so slightly, and he wished more than anything to be able to throw that blame at her. They hadn't known what to look for because *she* had refused to tell them. Even just knowing what charms to look for would have helped, surely, but instead, they'd had to risk everyone's life and almost forfeit the curse to find it. He had half a mind to say all of that to the enchantress. But Luna spoke before he was able.

"You have always seen the world in a unique way. Your dreams guided your heart. However, you were able to find them didn't matter. What mattered was that you found them. And just in time.

"You have done very well, Syrena. I apologize for putting such a burden on you to keep this curse for so many years from such a young age. Being stuck inside, having to navigate this without your mother to help you, made it all the harder, and I can never apologize enough for the circumstances of your trial, but the magic that suppresses the darkness required one with a pure heart. Otherwise, they would be consumed by it. You have proven your heart to be pure, and it is my honor to present you with the White Light."

Hunter watched as Luna reached her hands out towards Syrena. Hunter tightened his grip on her, ready to pull her out of harm's way should it be needed. In Luna's outstretched hands, beams of white light collected, until a substantial sized ball rested in her palms.

"It is for you to accept," the glowing woman said.

Hunter watched as Syrena strained to look at the orb, then glanced in his direction, as if asking for his approval. Despite his own reservations and hesitations about the matter, he knew that this wouldn't hurt her. This was and always would be what she was meant to do. He smiled and gave her a nod of encouragement. Syrena let go of his hand, leaving his fingers cold and anxiety hammering in his chest, and stepped forward to receive the orb of light. Hunter watched as she slowly lifted the orb from Luna's hands.

"I accept," was her soft reply.

The minute the words were out of her mouth, Syrena was engulfed in light, and lifted off the floor as she had been only moments before. Luna stood inside the bubble with her, on the floor, watching the events unfold with a smile. Fear tangled in Hunter's stomach as he rushed towards them, only to be pushed back by the glowing ball. He yelled out her name, pushing forward against the shield, but it wouldn't budge. He could do nothing but watch as the light from the orb pierced her chest.

"Syrena!" he screamed, slamming his fists against the glowing barrier as his view of Syrena became completely obstructed. Panic welled within him. He had no idea if she was dead or alive, if she was in pain. What was he going to do if they had done everything they were supposed to, then at the final step, she was killed? The thought only made him fight harder.

He punched the wall as hard as he could, screaming her name, until his hands made contact with nothing.e He fell forward towards Syrena, who stood on the ground exactly where she had been only a moment before. She was smiling, a faint glow fading from her skin as she reopened her eyes and focused on Luna.

Hunter did his best to swallow his fear, watching with wide eyes as Luna said, "You are free to live your life as you choose. Free to leave the manor and return as you see fit."

Luna then turned to the rest of them. "Protect your princess. The four signs are called to protect the Keeper of the White Light from darkness here and beyond. The princess, in return, protects her people with love and devotion. That's how it has been, and how it must always stay."

The others nodded to Luna while Hunter returned to Syrena's side as calmly as he could, scanning her for injury or harm. When he found none, he reclaimed her hand with his, smiled, and said, "With my life, if I must."

Luna turned to Hunter and Syrena . "Take care of each other. You are strong together. Never forget that." Then she was gone, disappearing into the light, the same way that she had appeared.

Her disappearance seemed to break a tension that held the other signs in place. Austyn and Jupiter came running to Syrena; Jupiter had tears streaming down her face.

"I'm so happy! We did it! You're free!" Jupiter sobbed.

"Thank you," Syrena said, her voice thick with her own tears, "for helping me." Hunter couldn't help but squeeze her hand. When she was finished hugging her two friends, she stood back and addressed the whole group. "This manor is too big for just me. You're all welcome to stay."

Hunter tuned out of the conversation then, as everyone figured out who was staying where. He hadn't thought about going home since he'd arrived. He'd been so caught up in helping Syrena and the signs, that thoughts of his dad hadn't even crossed his mind since that first meeting, when he'd seen that Syrena was real. Now, he had something serious to consider. Was he ready to go home?

He hadn't felt more like he belonged anywhere than he did when he was with Syrena and the other signs. Did he want to sacrifice that comfort to return home, be forced back into the foundation, to forget that this adventure, and his purpose in life, didn't exist?

By the time Syrena had gotten confirmation from the others in the group that they would remain in the manor with her, Hunter knew what his answer was going to be. He didn't belong anywhere else but here with them.

Syrena looked up at him and seemed to see his answer in his eyes, because she smiled. He vowed that he never wanted to see anything but that smile on her face for the rest of the time that they spent together.

Chapter Seven: Returning to Normal

The first week after Syrena accepted the White Light, those in the house were unsure of what to do. Hunter spent a lot of that time watching as Syrena flitted about, hosting for her houseguests and trying to make sure that there was always something for them to do, to eat, to entertain themselves with, or to pay attention to. With the curse going on, there hadn't been much actual entertaining that she'd needed to do, but now, she was entirely in lady of the manor mode, making sure that every need was met.

Gone were the late night snacks in the study or the early mornings in the den. Now it was breakfast in the dining hall, game night in front of the fire. He hadn't seen her this happy, or exhilarated, since the Christmas party she'd thrown all those months ago.

It was magnificent, to watch the way that she fell into her caregiving role, but Hunter also found it sad. He knew that it was something she had done out of habit—and perhaps out of boredom—because of so many years spent locked inside the manor. Even with her newfound freedom, Syrena seldom asked to go outside, save for the evening, when she and Hunter would step out onto the balcony of her room to watch the sunset—something she'd rarely been able to do in her mad rush to get indoors for all those years. So many years, she'd spent just watching it from inside the doors. But, Hunter ceded, she had been right about the view. It was much more beautiful than the one he'd had in his room when he'd first started staying here.

The other thing that took Hunter by surprise was how much he truly hadn't cherished his life as an only child before being forced into the house with other people. Jupiter and Austyn bickered every chance that they were given, even in regard to things that shouldn't have required an argument. Hunter was utterly astounded by the arguments that they got into. Syrena found it amusing, while Phoenix tuned it out, claiming that his oldest and youngest siblings had been the same way back home. Hunter, however, could do nothing but bare witness and worry that the two wouldn't go for each other's throats if someone did not step in. It luckily never seemed to escalate that far.

As they all started to settle into the routine of the household, however, Hunter did his best to encourage Syrena to step away from the hosting role a bit more and start to truly merge with the group. Hunter wanted more than anything to help her take her steps toward freedom, but he couldn't bring himself to force her. After so many years inside this house, it truly was all she knew, and Hunter knew that it would take time before she was ready to venture away from that safety—especially after all of the changes that had come their way in the last year.

He started small, by helping her to cook dinner instead of allowing her to do everything on her own. The others slowly started to follow suit, helping with the dishes or setting and clearing the table. Even with the servants still in the manor, doing much of the heavy lifting when it came to chores and tasks, Syrena and the others did what they could to function with each other. They were, for all intents and purposes, a family. It was strange for Hunter to see that, to feel that, in such a positive and comforting light— from the reactions of the others on most nights, he figured they might feel the same too.

It wasn't just around the house, though, that Hunter helped make Syrena feel more like one of them. She had been clear the few times he'd asked that she wasn't ready to go beyond the manor grounds yet, but she did allow him to take her outside to the gardens—to sit with her that first night they stayed out after sunset in the grass. She'd been so tense, so afraid, until the sun slipped low beyond the horizon... and nothing happened.

It was only after they were sure, after her shoulders had dropped and she'd leaned into him, that the others had slipped outside to join them. It was the most peaceful his life had been.

Sure, as the days continued on and the year mark of when he'd left home came and went, he thought of his parents, of his mother specifically, and wondered how she was—wondered if she still thought of him and worried. He thought about writing her a letter, had sat in the library a dozen times and considered what he would say—but always decided against it. What do you say to a woman who never supported saying not even a whisper to her for over a year? After not bothering to call, text, or even write a letter, if people even did that anymore?

He was afraid to break his own heart as much as he was to break hers.

These were the thoughts that kept him up most nights. Now that the White Light was in Syrena's care, he spent more time thinking about home. His task had been completed. He was content, happy. He had everything, even a family.

But he had still left his own family behind. So when he was quiet, when he was alone, he wondered.

On one particularly difficult night for sleep, Syrena found him hidden away in the back corner of the library with a book splayed out across his lap—though he was more so looking out the window than actually reading it.

"Something on your mind?" Syrena asked softly as she came to sit across from him.

He turned to her, offering her a small smile as he closed the book and set it aside. "Nothing important," he murmured.

Syrena tilted her head inquisitively. "You've been spending a lot of time in here lately. Maybe more than when we were hunting down answers."

Hunter nodded. "Just trying to get more of an understanding of all of this."

He gestured vaguely to the room, trying his best to indicate everything that had happened. It wasn't a lie, but he still felt like he wasn't being honest, and his hand went up to worry his earring—or where his earring used to be. He'd refused to wear it since breaking the curse nearly a month before . "Seems like we did what we were supposed to but have no better of an understanding of what we did, why we did it, or how it all fits together."

He'd been reading the books in here one by one, trying to see if her father had left any indication behind about her powers, about the White Light, but there was nothing so far as he could tell.

Syrena sighed deeply and looked out the window. "I don't blame you for that," she murmured. "Sometimes I wonder if this all was a big hallucination. But then I know you were there to witness it too, so how could it be? Then I start to think that maybe I've made all of you up, too, after being alone for so long . . ." Syrena glanced at him out of the corner of her eye.

Hunter chuckled and leaned forward, taking her hand and pulling her to stand before him. His hands rested on the outside of her thighs as she looked down at him and he held those crystal blue eyes. "You mean to tell me that you made up four other people, all of whom dreamed about you, and then hallucinated glowing lights, backstories for all of us, and a glowing woman who made you a princess of this entire realm—with superpowers?"

Syrena merely shrugged. "It almost makes more sense than the truth."

Hunter stood, still smiling at her, and leaned down to press a very tentative kiss onto her lips. They had only kissed a handful of times since their first one after she'd been unconscious when the curse broke, and every time Hunter kissed her like it was the first time—too afraid that it could be their last.

Syrena's cheeks flushed as he pulled away and she looked down.

"Does it seem like you're hallucinating?" he said softly.

Syrena shook her head. "I suppose not."

Hunter chuckled again, then pulled her into a hug.

For a long moment, they were silent, then Syrena asked softly, "Why did you come?"

Hunter's brows pulled together. "I'm sorry?"

"Why did you come after you started having the dreams? I know all of you had them and all of you came, but I feel like I can't ask the others. But with you . . . why did you come?" She pulled away and looked at him.

Hunter sighed. "I dreamt you were in danger, that you needed help, needed me. So, I came."

"But how did you know that I was even real?"

"I didn't. But after so many years of dreaming about you, I had to take the risk." Hunter shrugged, suddenly embarrassed by his admission.

"Years?" Syrena's expression changed to one of genuine shock at his admission..

Hunter nodded. "I was twelve the first time I had a dream about you, Syrena."

Syrena looked out the window , a faraway look in her eyes. "That was when my mother died," she said softly. "When my father chose not to tell me the truth about all of this."

"The connection ran deep, so when you woke me from dreams in fear and tears, I knew I had to come. No matter what it took." Hunter sighed. " Let me ask you this, princess," he watched as she frowned at the title, "How did you know to look for me? For any of us?"

Syrena shook her head. "I didn't know to look for the others." She spun back to face him, still so close that her eyes twinkled in the moonlight. "I only knew to look for you." Pink twinged her cheeks again as she turned away. "I would have this dream that I was sitting on a beach facing the sea, and someone would come up to me and hand me a yellow rose. I could always feel this warmth, this purity coming from the person. It was like we were right there together. Perhaps since those dreams started, I could feel this... this pull, like someone far away was tapping on my shoulder . But I could never touch the rose. They would try to hand it to me, but as soon as I would go to reach for it, I would wake up. All I ever knew was to look for gray eyes.

"Then suddenly, the dreams shifted. About a year ago, I started seeing different things. We would meet at a bus stop, or we would be in my garden, not on the beach. I would see snippets of us touching hands or having conversations, but I could never quite hear anything. It was all just out of reach. Then the pull started to move. It got stronger the closer you got, I think. When you were at the party, the sensation was almost overwhelming. When we locked eyes, it felt like—" She cut off, her cheeks flushing again with embarrassment. Hunter thought she was so beautiful with the rose color on her cheeks.

"It felt like what?" he pressed softly, cupping her cheek.

"It felt like everything was snapping into place," she answered, nestling her face into his palm.

"Syrena, I—"

But he was cut off by Nyx's voice in the doorway.

"Sorry to break up whatever moment you guys are having in here, but you're going to want to come down to the living room." His eyes were wide, his breathing a little too quick.

Syrena and Hunter exchanged a glance, then followed him back into the main part of the house.

Chapter Eight: The Threat

Luna was standing by the hearth when they entered the living room. Jupiter sat on the couch across from her, a mug of tea in a death grip in her hands, while Austyn sat in the chair on the opposite side of the room.

Nyx settled into the couch next to Jupiter as Hunter and Syrena slowed to a stop in the doorway. Luna's attention turned fully on them as her lips curved into a soft smile.

"Syrena," Luna said.

"Luna," Syrena returned, but she said it hesitantly.

Hunter didn't blame her. Not once since she'd left them after the curse was broken did he think they'd see the apparition again—especially not this soon.

"What are you doing here?" Hunter asked cautiously.

When Luna's smile turned tight, Hunter looked to the others to see if they could clue him in, but all three shook their heads.

"Why don't you sit?" Luna gestured toward the furniture with a hand, the glow from which cast an illusion of lighting the path to the seat.

Syrena followed the instruction, but Hunter merely stood behind Syrena's chair, ready to angle himself between the two women should anything that he didn't like start to happen.

Once Syrena was settled, Luna's attention expanded from her to all of them in the room. "I'm sorry to have dropped in on all of you so unexpectedly, and so soon after you've just gained your peace. Something has come to my attention that needs to be delivered as soon as possible and directly to you all."

Syrena reached over her shoulder with her hand, fingers splayed as Hunter grasped it. Her grip was deadly tight and fearful.

Luna's attention turned back to Syrena. "The Dark Keeper has learned that the White Light is now back in the hands of the Light Keeper—you, Syrena. The Dark Keeper learned that the light has reawakened, meaning that their powers will be challenged and suppressed, and they are coming for you in order to gain their full power back and then some. They wish to take it for themselves and turn it against us."

Syrena's grip tightened, fueling the anger that swelled now in Hunter's chest.

"Why is this the first we're hearing of Dark Keeper?" Hunter asked, not bothering to hide his anger. "We were told to break a curse, to protect her, to make sure she was able to keep the White Light thriving. We were never told that there was a real *threat*."

Luna's gaze, slow and ethereal as always, turned to him. "All things in nature come in balance, Hunter. Where there is light, there must also be darkness. The Dark Keeper has been dormant for many, many years. Through her mother's years, and her grandmother's before that. They have not been a threat in many, many years."

"Then why are they a threat now? Why is it our problem?" Austyn cut in.

"I don't know, child. That is for you as the signs to figure out."

Luna's light began to fade and flicker.

"Wait, you can't just come in here and tell us someone is coming for Syrena, coming to potentially kill her, with no information on how to prevent it."

"Syrena should know what she's to do." She faded further.

"My mother died before she could teach me anything, Luna. I don't even truly know what the White Light *is*."

"You do know, child. Everything that you need to know has been given to you. You just need to look within."

Before they could ask any further questions, she was gone, leaving the room with nothing but the crackle of the fire to break the tension and the silence.

71

Chapter Nine: The Journey of the Signs

None of them got much sleep that night, if Hunter's night was any indication to go by—as well as the bloodshot eyes and permeating silence the next morning at breakfast. Syrena had slept in her own room, but she'd gripped his hand as soon as she'd seen him that morning and had refused to let it go since. She had been mostly quiet, though, and he thought it best not to push her. This reveal meant a lot to every one of them, but it directly affected her. If they were coming for the White Light...they were coming for her.

The room was so quiet, so oddly tense, that when Syrena began speaking toward the end of the meal, Hunter saw all of them jump.

"So, I've been thinking since yesterday." Syrena began slowly, as if testing the words. When she saw that they were all looking at her, though, she seemed to gain confidence and push forward. "I know that we have all just been starting to get settled in here with one another, but it seems like it might be time for us to start moving again."

Hunter watched as Austyn's brows furrowed and Jupiter's brows rose to her hairline. Phoenix's arms crossed over his chest as he settled back against his chair to listen. He was the most stoic of the group, always the first to listen, the longest to stay quiet, the last to offer his insights. Hunter appreciated the steadiness that he brought to the chaos that came from the rest of them.

"What do you mean?" Jupiter asked softly, glancing at Hunter, then to the other boys at the table, before returning her gaze to Syrena.

"Yeah, why now? When, you know, there could be people chasing us?" Austyn asked..

"It's just . . . My mother was supposed to teach me about being the White Light, but she never got the chance to pass down that knowledge. Instead of embracing what she was, what *I* am, my father buried that part of our history away. Essentially, we don't know anything about any of this." She gestured generally, working to get the point across.

"Why do we need to know?" Austyn said

"Because if we *don't* know, when the people that Luna says are coming get here, then we're going to be wholly unprepared," Hunter said, meeting Austyn's stare—a challenge.

Austyn's attention turned back to Syrena. "So how do you expect us to get the information we're missing when the one person who knew all of it can't give it to us anymore?" To his credit, Austyn's tone softened, his face sympathetic, as he asked the last part.

Syrena looked to Hunter, eyes showing her uncertainty despite the rigidness of her spine. He nodded for her to continue. She could do this. She dipped her chin slightly in response and then turned back to their friends.

"I think we need to venture away from the manor. Visit anyone who might know anything about what the signs are supposed to do, what the White Light is supposed to be or represent." She glanced at each of them respectively.

"You want us to talk to our families," Nyx said, eyebrows furrowing in confusion, and something that looked almost like anger colored the edge of his voice as he continued. "Families that we don't talk to," he directed that at Hunter specifically, who fought the urge to flinch, "or families that we don't have?" The last part had his attention back on Syrena, but it was Jupiter who dropped her gaze to her lap.

Syrena said nothing, but her eyes turned sorrowful.

"My family isn't gonna help with this," Austyn said, offering a cold, humorless smile. "They haven't gone farther west than Pennsylvania. They've never left American soil. What makes you think they flew half-way around the world to help a girl they never knew over a cross bracelet charm that glows once in a while?"

"You did." Syrena crossed her arms.

Hunter could tell that her patience was wearing thin.

Austyn glared.

Hunter glared back. *Why was he being such a jerk about this?*

"So, you think our families might know something about all of this?" Jupiter asked, her voice soft and full of pain.

"Syrena's mom was the last keeper," Hunter said, "meaning that the last generation of signs—the people who gave us these charms—weren't completely blind to the power that they, or she, had. My guess is that, at the very least, they knew something. Why they kept the significance of these charms from us when they gave them to us, I don't really know, but if my parents are any model to go by, they kept it from us for a reason, that reason being that they didn't want us to come here. I'd like to know why that is."

Hunter shrugged as casually as he could, but inside, something stirred—a mixture of anger and anxiety at the thought of seeing his parents, in hindsight. *How much did they know when his dad spoke of my dreams? Did my dad know what he did when he gifted me his earring? Was my dad truly so naïve to think that Syrena's mother was the last to hold this power? So selfish to think that I wouldn't follow the call? To think I would've been able to resist it if these were the forces driving this all along?*

Hunter forced the tornado of questions to the back of his mind. There would be time for them when he got back home. For now, his job was to be at Syrena's side for whatever she needed—even if it meant, in this moment, convincing the rest of the signs that this was the best and only option in order for them to move forward.

"Maybe they have no idea." Austyn leaned forward onto the table. "Her mother wasn't kept inside like Syrena was. She wasn't cursed, so far as that indicates. Didn't anyone ever think to ask that? Maybe there were no signs back then. Skipped a generation or something."

Hunter saw Syrena glance at him from the corner of his eye, but his gaze fixed to Austyn. "That's still worth asking about. Maybe they still passed the story down in case, then when they never got called, they thought it myths and legends and let it go. We don't live in an age that embraces fantasy anymore."

Austyn scoffed, sitting back in his chair. "You don't believe that."

"I believe that someone somewhere has to know something, Austyn, and this is the only lead we have." Hunter's gaze turned pleading.

Hunter felt Syrena's gaze leave him as she turned back to face the group. "I know that this is a lot, but if there's something that we're missing regarding all of this White Light stuff, then I feel like we need to know it. Don't you?"

"I don't have anyone to ask about my sign, Syrena," Jupiter said, looking almost as if she were on the verge of tears. "How are we supposed to find out about mine?"

Hunter saw Syrena's features soften as she glanced over at the young girl. "Is there not someone from your hometown that would know something?" Syrena asked softly.

Jupiter shrugged her shoulders. "I have some uncles that I see for the holidays, but they don't come around much beyond that anymore. Perhaps my mother or father told them something before . . ." She trailed off, but the tears that welled in her eyes said the rest.

"You've searched the study?" Phoenix asked.

"We're going to look through the libraries here with fresh eyes, but my father wiped anything to do with the keeper, the White Light, and the curse from our house after my mother died. Her history, my history...it's gone. This is the only chance that we have of being prepared for whatever is coming for us...for me." Syrena's eyes were filled with sadness as she looked at Nix. "My father was determined in his last years to help me, to make it right, but he fell ill before we made much progress."

Phoenix nodded. "Then I'm with you that learning as much as we can will benefit all of this. If there's nothing here that's going to help us, then we'll have to follow the only lead we have: our families." He glanced down the table to Austyn, who was staring off to the far corner of the room and avoiding all of their sideways glances.

Syrena let out a deep breath, glancing over at Hunter, who was already looking at her and nodding. "Okay," she said with what Hunter knew was forced cheer. "Then we start there. After breakfast, we can try to figure out how to go about that, in a way that makes the most sense, and then we can start to pack. I suspect that this will take several weeks, so if there's anything that we need to do to prepare, then we can take the next few days to do it, but the sooner we can get on the road, the better it will be.

"If there's anything that you all can think of over the next few days about how you were gifted your signs—any information or something that seems significant now in hindsight—please share it. At this point, there isn't really any information that could hurt, only help."

The others nodded—all except Austyn, who finally turned back to face them.

"What if we do all this traveling and nothing comes of it?" he asked.

Syrena sighed. "I suppose that we'll discuss that if it happens. But for now, let's just hope that it doesn't."

"It'll help more than it'll hurt," Phoenix added, leaning forward . "Anything we learn at this point will benefit us. Even if it's something we consider to be bad, it's more information than we had before. Plus, I've always wanted to travel anyway." He finished with a wry smile.

Hunter offered him a half-smile of thanks.

"I'm in," Jupiter said. "Even if we don't find out much from my family, it'll be nice to see them again . . . to be able to tell them what's happened." Her smile was sad, but her eyes twinkled. Hunter's smile turned to one of sympathy as Syrena reached across the table to offer her a supportive squeeze of the fingers. "And I mean, we all keep talking about how much we want to see Jersey."

Syrena beamed at her, the thankfulness for her attempt at humor evident on her face.

All of the eyes at the table then turned to Austyn.

"I wasn't prepared to traipse all over the world for this job, you know." His tone was more falsely annoyed than really annoyed as he shot a glare at all of them, and Hunter knew that his outer shell was cracking, even if just a little.

"You already did traipse all over the world for this," Jupiter pointed out, snickering.

"Watch it," Hunter warned, glancing between the two of them. "We're just trying to do what's best for all of us. None of us truly understand what happened when we broke the curse. Plus, we don't know where to go from here, so we're just looking for answers."

Austyn turned his glare on the blond-haired man. "Do I have a choice?"

"Yes," Hunter said lowly, "but it would be a lot better if we were all on the same page with this."

"Please, Austyn," Syrena pleaded from his side.

Austyn glanced between the two of them and sighed, dropping his head. "Whatever." In a sharp movement, he pushed himself away from the table, standing to his full height. "If there's nothing else you'll be imposing on me, I think I'm due for a nap."

He left without another word.

The others shared glances for a long moment, then Syrena cleared her throat. "Well, that went better than I expected... honestly."

Jupiter snorted. "Don't let him get under your skin, Syrena. It's just, you know, *boys*."

Syrena giggled as both Hunter and Phoenix chorused a whiney, "Hey," into the room. Jupiter giggled too as the two girls gathered the breakfast plates and scurried into the kitchen to clean up.

LATER THAT AFTERNOON, the group met in the study to plot out their travel route and to begin making plans for what they would need for their travels. Phoenix and Jupiter contributed actively, trying to suggest things they would need and what path would work best, but Austyn stayed back, observing more than contributing.

While Syrena sat and talked with the others, Hunter retreated to the corner of the room, where Austyn stood, staring out the window.

"I'm not in the mood to talk," Austyn said lowly.

"Well, then you can listen for a minute." Hunter came up beside his friend and then crossed his arms, glancing out over the garden behind the house. "Coming here to help Syrena was my saving grace. It let me get away from parents who wanted me to live out their dreams, rather than my own. The idea of going back to them isn't my favorite."

"So why do it?" Austyn turned to Hunter, the anger in his eyes only thinly veiled. "You know as well as I do that parents like ours won't give us anything worth salt that will help us."

Hunter sighed. "Because this is what she wants, Austyn, and we're supposed to be helping her. If this Dark Keeper comes and we don't know what we're up against—or what we're working with—they could take everything we just worked so hard to get for her...or worse."

Austyn shook his head, turning back to the window. "I came out here to figure out why I was dreaming about a girl, why this girl was screaming for help. I came out here to get away from the pressure of being the disappointment of the family. Lotta pressure to get a trade job and make a lot of money and get a good wife. Pop out some kids and settle down. That wasn't the life I wanted for myself, and it was hard to live with the side eyes and the backhanded comments. Got out the first chance I got, you know? I didn't ever have the intention of going back."

"Even if it will help? Even if it helps you achieve that goal of saving her?"

Austyn turned a pleading glance to him.

"We owe it to her."

Austyn shook his head and turned away, saying nothing.

After several minutes, Hunter just clapped him on the shoulder, reminiscent of the first time they'd met over a year ago at the bus station, when this had all first begun.

"Just give it an honest thought, okay? Just because we go back, it doesn't mean we have to stay. At least, that's what I've been telling myself." As Hunter said it, he realized that it was true. His worry about returning home was quelled slightly by the promise that they would come back to the manor once it was done.

Austyn nodded but did not turn. Hunter took that as his cue to return to the rest of the group.

He took his post next to Syrena at the head of the group, who smiled up at him briefly before returning her attention back to their friends to continue their planning. At some point, Austyn came over and sat on the back of Phoenix's chair, sharing only a passing glance with Hunter, who couldn't help but smile.

If this was all the progress he could make, he decided, then he had done a good job.

It was well into the night by the time Syrena sat back and smiled. "Alright, then. We have a plan."

"Phoenix and Jupiter will head to Phoenix's old place to go through what is in storage, try to find the journals from his family," Syrena recounted from a piece of paper in front of her.

"I can't make any promises that I'll find anything.," Nyx said slowly. "Remember that my father ditched us when I was young and my mother hasn't responded to a message in who knows how long. I've been on my own for years. So, I'm grasping at straws here."

Syrena nodded. "We're just grateful for you to be willing to try."

Phoenix offered a half smile in response.

"From there, the two of them will head to France to try to get information from Jupiter's uncles," Syrena continued.

"But the same stipulations are in place," Jupiter said. "I don't know how much they know, if anything."

"That's okay," Hunter said. "We're at a dead end so whatever we can find is a step forward at this point."

"While they're doing that," Syrena wrapped up, "Hunter and I will go back to England to talk to his parents, see what they know."

Hunter nodded. "At this point in time, they seem like our best lead, since my dad is alive and was the one that gave this thing to me, but he's stubborn and was adamantly against me coming here, so who knows if he'll be willing to tell me anything?"

Syrena lay a comforting hand on his arm, then turned to Austyn. "That just leaves your family and where you fit into this. We think the best bet is for you to go with Jupiter and Nyx. If we all come up blank, we'll meet back here at the house, then head across to America for your family together as a team. But it's up to you."

Austyn shook his head. "I think I need to go back alone, find out what they know by myself. If I show up with you lot on their front steps, I won't get anything from them."

Jupiter punched him in the arm.

"Hey!" he said, scowling.

"'*You lot*,'" she muttered with a scowl of her own.

Hunter rolled his eyes.

"Are you sure you want to do this, Austyn?" Syrena asked softly.

Another look passed between Hunter and Austyn—one of understanding, of thanks and grace—and he nodded. "If it'll help, I'll do it. But I'm doin' it my way. Alone, on my time. So, I'll be there for a bit."

Syrena smiled gratefully and nodded. "We understand. Just...don't forget to keep us updated?"

He nodded, dropping their gazes to look at the floor. "I'll keep in touch."

"Alright. Then it's settled. We'll take the next few days to pack and prepare, then we'll split up and see what we can figure out about this whole big mess." Syrena forced another smile, one that barely hid the uncertainty and fear Hunter knew stirred within her. But the rest returned her gesture.

Then, unsure of what else to do, they slowly dispersed, trickling off to their rooms to contemplate what they'd just agreed to do.

Chapter Ten: Preparing for Travel

The night before they were set to depart the manor, Hunter couldn't sleep. Too many thoughts were going through his head. Who were these Dark Keepers? How much time did they have? What risk were they at?

There were also selfish thoughts too, about what he would find when he got home. Would his parents have any concern for what he'd done in the past year? Were they worried about him? Did they care that he'd left, or had they moved on?

Part of him didn't want to care what they thought—especially with the new impending threat of the Dark Keeper—but the other part was he was still their son, and he wanted to know that they still loved him, that they still cared. Still worried.

Hunter sighed at the ceiling for what felt like the millionth time and rolled over again, trying to find a comfortable spot on the mattress but failing. The clock on the nightstand read well past one in the morning, and he contemplated giving up on sleep entirely, given that they had agreed to meet in the foyer at eight, and he didn't know exactly what their travels would have in store in terms of accommodations or when the next time sleep might come—so this could be his last chance for a while.

With a groan, Hunter grabbed the pillow from under his head and shoved it over his eyes and ears. Maybe if he could block out all light and sound . . .

On the verge of throwing the pillow off his face, a knock came at the door. He pulled the pillow away from his face and rested it beside him, adjusting himself against the headboard into a sitting position. "Come in," he called to the person at the door.

The door swung open to reveal Syrena, backlit by the dim lights in the hallway as she stepped inside and then closed the door.

"I hope I didn't wake you," she said softly.

"No," Hunter murmured. "Couldn't sleep."

"Me neither. I'm worried about tomorrow. About...everything." She hovered in the doorway hesitantly, as if unsure.

"Me too. But tell me why you are." Hunter reached forward and patted the bed by his feet, inviting her to sit.

She approached the bed quietly, watching her feet instead of him as she took each step, her nightgown swishing around her shins. Hesitating with each movement, Syrena pulled herself up onto the bed, sitting with her legs over the side, back straight.

"It feels so silly," she said, still looking at her hands clasped in her lap.

"I doubt it's as silly as you think it is," Hunter said softly, trying to be supportive and encouraging.

Syrena laughed with little humor. "I'm sure it is, especially to someone like you."

Hunter's brows furrowed but he said nothing. He was sure she didn't mean the undercut of the words she'd spoken, so he waited for her to be ready to explain.

After a long moment, that explanation came.

Syrena sighed, then pressed on. "It's just that . . . It's just that I haven't left this manor in so many years. I mean, we left to go find Phoenix when we realized that he wasn't going to come to us back when we were breaking the curse, but everything surrounding that was in such a flurry that I didn't even think about it at the time. But now all I can do is think about it. And this isn't even just leaving the manor. We'll be leaving Ireland and there's a threat *again,* even though I thought this was all over and . . . It's a lot."

Hunter nodded. "It is a lot. None of that is silly, Syrena."

Syrena laughed again. "But it *is* so silly. People in their twenties are supposed to want to leave home. It's normal."

Now it was Hunter's turn to laugh. "Normal people in their twenties don't have superpowers or villains chasing after them, or curses. When you find something that's normal about any of this situation, I beg you to please inform the rest of us."

She smiled at him through the darkness, the dim moonlight from the window catching against her teeth, which even illuminated minimally, emphasized her beauty.

"Speaking of not normal," Hunter said, his thoughts lingering on something that had triggered her mention of twenties. "Can I ask you something?"

Syrena nodded, her eyes open and honest as they turned back to him, and he couldn't help but gulp.

"In one of the dreams that I had about you, you were with Luna, and she mentioned that you'd aged a year overnight, from being late to the manor. Is that . . . Is that true?"

Syrena had looked away as soon as he'd begun to ask, and he'd lost his nerve. But he also knew that he needed an answer. He needed to understand more of this, as much as he could, before they went away.

"It's true," she said softly after a long time. "One night, I was out after the sunset, and I came back inside to find Luna here, ready to dole out the punishment. I learnt quickly to never play with the curse after that." She laughed humorlessly. "But that was when I moved into my room—with the sunsets— where I could always watch them, admire them, even if I couldn't be outside to see them."

Hunter reached out and touched her hand where it rested on the bedspread. "Did it happen more than once?"

She shook her head. "Only that one time. About the time when my father got really sick. I was out in the garden looking for comfort and lost track of time." She shrugged, then smiled sadly at him.

"So you're actually older than twenty-one?" Hunter asked.

She shook her head. "The age you have is right. It's a little convoluted on the back end, though. No one here knew about the time-jump because they found out about the curse after my father died. By then, I was too afraid to tell him and cause more stress. So, on my eighteenth birthday—the year I really turned nineteen—I managed to tell them I was nineteen and pass it off as them missing a birthday from grief and stress over my father's illness. No one's ever questioned it."

Hunter tilted his head. "Haven't some of them been here since you were born?"

Syrena's responding laugh was musical. "That's a blessing in disguise. Some have been here so long that the years truly have blurred together, and they forget that I am no longer a child." She shrugged. "I don't like lying, but it's sometimes easier than explaining."

Hunter nodded, still not having let go of her hand.

"I'm really scared of what's to come."

"Me too," he said, squeezing her fingers

Syrena flipped her hand over on the blankets and returned the gesture. They stayed like that for a long moment before she broke the silence. "What about you? Why are you still up?"

Hunter shrugged. "I can never sleep the night before I travel."

Syrena rolled her eyes, a gesture he could see even in the dark—maybe even feel. "Hunter."

"Truly," he said, throwing his hands up in defense. "Traveling makes me anxious. Add into the mix a little family drama and impending doom and it makes the perfect anti-sleep cocktail."

Syrena cocked her head. "Do you want to talk about it?"

Hunter shook his head. "Aren't we supposed to be your support team, princess?"

"As my sign, perhaps. But as my boyfriend, that's a two-way street."

The word hung heavy in the air between them, and Hunter wanted so badly to hark on it—to ask her to say it again, to confirm it, to verify that he'd heard it. But by the smile that spread on her face as soon as she said it, he knew he was right, and he knew better than to try to ruin the moment.

"Perhaps another night then, princess." Hunter grasped her fingers again and pulled them to his mouth to kiss. "It's late and you need your rest."

Syrena sighed. "This once, I'll let it slide."

He chuckled. "Gracious as ever."

Syrena stood and leaned forward, replacing the press of her fingers with the press of her lips to his, then retreated to the door. "I'll see you in the morning, Hunter."

She was gone before he could reply.

HE MUST HAVE FALLEN asleep at some point after she left, because the next thing that Hunter knew, the alarm clock was ringing. He groaned, fighting the sleep that wanted nothing more than to drag him under once more, then quickly got dressed to join the rest of his friends in the kitchen. They were to see Phoenix and Jupiter off first, then head out themselves. Austyn would leave sometime after them.

The entire manor was already in a flurry of activity by the time Hunter emerged from his room. Even from the hallway, he could hear Austyn and Jupiter fighting in the kitchen while Syrena tried to mediate. There was even a distinct silence where he knew Phoenix sat in all that chaos.

In the hallway by the door, he knew that some of those that worked throughout the manor were working to gather the belongings for the trip so it would be easier for them to pack into the taxis that would arrive around half past eight.

Hunter quickly made his way to the kitchen to see what the ruckus was about and found everyone gathered, already up in arms. A smile found its way to his face.

"Good morning, everyone. It sounds like we're all in the perfect mood to begin our travels."

Austyn and Jupiter glared at him almost immediately while Syrena shot him a pleading look. Phoenix just shared a sly smirk, which he assumed was meant for either him or the entire group.

"Lady Syrena," a voice said from the opposite doorway, distracting their attention before the situation could escalate further.

The entire room turned to face the butler—Gerald. Hunter had learned his name in the year since the party.

He dipped slightly at the waist, then continued. "A car has pulled up to the front for you."

Syrena nodded her thanks and Gerald returned the way he had come. "That's Nyx and Jupiter's car, so ours shouldn't be far behind, Hunter."

The signs began to file out. Hunter went to follow suit but was quickly held back by Syrena's hand on his wrist. He turned to her, eyes full of concern.

"What is it?" he asked in a low voice as he registered the worry in her eyes.

"Promise me that no matter what happens and no matter what we find out, you're not going to leave me alone. That this, between you and I, means something." The panic in her eyes was something he hadn't been prepared for. It erased everything else—the worry of their travels, the faux annoyance at their friends' arguments, the tension that they all felt for having to return home, the impending danger of the Dark Keeper. This fear, he realized, was something she worried about more than anything else: being alone again.

Hunter grasped her hands and stepped forward, pressing a soft kiss to her forehead. "I promise that I'm not going anywhere, princess."

Syrena sighed, falling forward against his chest into his embrace. "Okay. Then let's get going."

Hunter pressed one more kiss to the crown of her head then released her, allowing her to lead the way into the foyer.

Syrena gave a heartfelt goodbye to the people that had worked for her for her entire life, hugging and kissing them and promising them she would return soon. After a final look for reassurance from Hunter, she approached the threshold and took a dramatic, very confident step outside.

Chapter Eleven: The Ferry

Their taxi pulled in a few minutes later to take them to the ferry. Hunter knew that Syrena was nervous, but he didn't push her as he helped the driver load the bags into the trunk, then settled in the backseat next to her. He tangled their fingers together in the middle seat and offered her hand a reassuring squeeze as the driver pulled away from the house, as she squeezed back. The tension in her body racketed up the farther they got from the manor. He watched as some of that anxiety gave way to excitement, to wonder as she took in, for the first time in he didn't quite know how many years, the area that surrounded her house. Her eyes flitted back and forth across the landscape quickly, taking in the hills she'd never seen from any angle other than from inside the manor, buildings she'd never been able to see even though she'd lived so close to them for so many years. He felt her hand relax from anxiety, then tighten again in wonder as the ocean came into view for the first time—perhaps the first time she had seen water like that, so vast and open.

Syrena's eyes were wide, her mouth slightly open as she panted at the scenery before her.

Hunter decided she had never looked more beautiful.

It didn't take long for them to reach the dock. As they approached, the driver informed them of where he'd have to let them off, as Syrena's wonder gave way to worry once again. Hunter knew it was because she would be leaving the confines of the car—leaving the safety of it all and stepping wholly and truly into the unknown for the first time.

"Do you trust me?" Hunter murmured as the car slowed to a stop.

Syrena looked at him, pupils wide in fear and confusion at his question, then nodded.

"Let me guide you through this, okay?"

Syrena's breath hitched. "How am I to get across the border?"

"You're a citizen of Ireland. You're welcome in any area under common travel laws. That's how I was able to travel to Ireland from England with such ease."

She nodded before he saw another question flit across her eyes.

"I'll answer all the questions you have, Syrena, but we have to go now, or we'll miss the ferry, okay?"

Syrena turned her attention away from him, out the windshield and toward the water where their boat bobbed lazily in the waves. "Alright," she murmured softly.

Hunter reached into his pocket to pay the taxi driver. Once they were square, he pressed a soft kiss to the side of her head in promise that the conversation wouldn't end there and then got out of the car with Syrena following. The cab drove off almost as soon as the bags were out of the trunk, leaving them standing on the gravel near the dock.

"What do we do now?" Syrena asked, genuine uncertainty in her voice as she took in their surroundings.

Hunter took the handles of their bags. "We have to get tickets over to the England port."

"Will that be hard?"

"No, princess." He offered her a reassuring smile then led her to the building off to the side of the dock.

As quickly as he could, he secured two tickets, then backed away from the booth.

"They're boarding now, so we can go onto the boat and find ourselves some seats. We don't leave for another hour though."

Syrena nodded absently, her attention already back on the ferry itself, sizing it up.

Hunter led the way to the ramp, making sure she was following every step of the way as they made their way up to the ferry, handed their tickets over, then worked their way inside, along with other passengers that were arriving.

"Hunter, it smells bad in here," Syrena said softly as they made their way into the middle of the boat, where rows of seats were lined up for passengers to sit for the journey.

Hunter only nodded in response and angled his path toward the stairs that led to the upper decks. It would be cold, he assumed, but it would at least have fresh air for her. It also had prettier views, and he wanted her to see them more than anything. They were traveling with purpose, that fact never escaped him, but if they were traveling, Hunter wanted her to get everything from it that she could. This would be the farthest she had ever gone from the manor, and he wanted her to see the world for all that it was—the beauty that was the ocean, the countryside, the oddity of the people that lived within it.

Syrena followed him up the stairs and then over to the benches he chose toward the edge, where she'd have a good view of the water and the horizon. He slid into the seat and placed their bags down, but Syrena wandered over to the railing to look out over the island that had been her home for so long, yet so closed off from her.

"It really is such a beautiful place," she said just loud enough for him to hear but not so loud that others might think her weird for saying it.

Hunter nodded even though she wasn't looking at him to see it. "Ireland is one of the most beautiful places I've ever seen," he replied, his eyes never leaving her.

As if she knew where his eyes truly were, her cheeks flushed with a blush, and she turned to look at him. "You're such a romantic, Hunter."

He only smiled softly at her in response, holding a hand out, inviting her to sit next to him, which she did.

"It may get cold up here, okay?"

She nodded, taking in the views around them as she leaned into him.

"Are you nervous still?" he asked softly.

"Yes. There isn't a single thing about this that doesn't worry me. Leaving home, what we might find, not finding anything, what it all could mean." She blushed again and then continued, "Meeting your parents."

Hunter couldn't help but chuckle at that. "You never cease to surprise me, princess."

Her smile curved her lips as her hand found his, locking their fingers together once more. "Aren't you nervous?"

Hunter shrugged with one shoulder. "Of course. But this needs to be done. We need to understand what your powers do, what they're for, and what roles the rest of us all play in this so we can protect you from whatever is coming."

Syrena leaned over and kissed him. "Thank you for doing this."

"It's my job as a sign," he answered.

She shook her head, smiling at him slyly, knowingly, but let him have his peace.

They sat in silence for the remainder of the time they were docked, Syrena watching the land around them with Hunter watching her. When the ferry finally blew its horn and signaled that they were pulling away, Syrena returned to the railing to watch, but Hunter remained seated, letting her enjoy this new experience. He knew this was bittersweet for her, discovering her home for the first time only to leave it on the same day, and he wanted her to experience those feelings in her own way. He knew that when she was ready, if she needed him, she would ask.

It didn't take long for the land to fade completely. Once out on the open water, Syrena returned to her seat, and then promptly fell asleep, the lack of sleep from the night before and the stress of the morning catching up with her. Despite his own exhaustion, Hunter remained awake, stroking her hair and keeping watch.

Despite it all, it was the most peaceful he had ever felt.

Chapter Twelve: The Journals

When the English coast came into view a few hours later, Hunter shook Syrena gently to wake her, not wanting her to miss a second. She was groggy at first, confused, but when she saw the greenery off the side of the ferry, he saw the excitement light inside of her. She looked to him with such joy and went to stand by the railing once more.

This time, he went with her, needing her support as he took in the coastline of his home country for the first time in nearly a year. Whether she knew he needed it or simply did it for herself, he didn't know, but Syrena wrapped her arms around his waist and held tightly, refusing to let go until the ferry had fully docked.

In that entire time, Hunter had so many thoughts, ranging from the excitement of Syrena seeing his home for the first time to the dread of being back on this soil and what his parents would think of him. There was anger and resentment there, living in the same vein as the fear of rejection he worried would come to him for not living up to his dad's expectations. No matter which way he spun it, he just didn't know what he was getting himself into.

But with her at his side, he decided he was going to be okay—and he would do whatever he needed to in order to make sure it was okay for her.

It was a long disembarking process as some people had to get down to the lower deck for their cars or find different modes of transport, Syrena and Hunter included. A bus was necessary to get them to the train station that would eventually bring them to Essex, Hunter's home.

Syrena clung tight to Hunter for the entirety of the transfers, from buying the bus ticket to boarding. Even on the bus, as they traipsed through the country, she gripped his arm, excitement and uncertainty warring with her. Hunter was grateful for the comfort as he continued to war with his own demons of doubt and dread. The closer they got to home, the more he began to think that this was the wrong choice.

They also hadn't heard anything from Jupiter or Nyx, even though it had been hours and they'd been in Ireland. He made a note to check in with them once they were on the train. All of them had cell phones now, part of the travel preparation process, with each of their numbers loaded so they could contact each other quickly if anything came up or went wrongIt was midday by the time they reached the train station, with the next train not departing until nightfall, so Hunter quickly bought them tickets while Syrena stretched her legs. When he returned, he suggested they go grab something to eat, which she agreed to quickly.

"I'm *starving*. But you'll have to recommend something good. Remember this is my first time in England," she said, glancing around then smiling brightly at him.

"What do you think of it so far?" he asked as he looped her hand over his arm, their bags safely stowed in a train station locker to wait for their ride later that night.

She shrugged. "It's so beautiful, but honestly, I have nothing to compare it to. All I've ever known are the manor grounds and walls. My first glimpses of the real world since I was a little girl happened today, and it's been so brief."

"Well," Hunter said, pressing a kiss to the side of her head in an attempt to drive off the sadness in her voice, "once all this is over, I'm hoping to change that, okay?"

Syrena nodded, beaming at him. She let him lead her into one of the restaurants close by. He only hoped he could give her a good recommendation and make it worth her while.

SYRENA ENDED UP GETTING fish and chips, laughing when Hunter shook his head and muttering, "Tourist," under his breath. Still, hearing her smile and laugh brought a warmth to him, and he tried—and failed—to take some of the chips off of her plate once the food came.

They ate and chatted about absolutely nothing the whole time, both seemingly grateful for the distraction from their task at hand. Soon, though—too soon for Hunter's liking—the food was gone, and the conversation lulled, as the reality of what they were doing truly set in for him.

He was heading home to see his family to tell them that he had found a girl he had dreamed about after not talking to them for a year. He hoped that they had information about a mythical set of powers and objects in order to protect them from another person with a mythical set of powers coming to potentially harm her. The absurdity of that information was clear to him and at the forefront of his mind—and the anxiety that came with that knowledge was nearly all-consuming.

It was also much simpler than that. It had been over a year since he'd been home, and he wasn't so sure that he was ready, try as he might, to convince himself that he was, to return home and face his dad, the fantastical elements aside. Would he be ready to face his dad's skepticism? Disappointment? Rage?

"Hunter?" Syrena asked quietly from beside him as they made their way back to the train station.

"Yes?" he replied, plastering a smile on his face and turning toward her.

"Are you okay?"

He nodded, leaning over to press a kiss to her cheek. "I'm okay."

She assessed his face for a long time, then gave him a hesitant smile. "Well, if that changes, you know you can talk to me."

He nodded again, then reached into his pocket and pulled out his phone. "I'm going to call the others and see if they've gotten anything so far."

The phone rang three times before Phoenix's voice came through clearly on the other side. "Yeah?"

Hunter couldn't help but snort. "That's how you always answer the phone?"

"Your name comes up when you call. That's why we put each other's numbers in before we left?"

Hunter shook his head then pressed on. "Have you guys found anything out yet?"

Phoenix sighed. "We're still at my old place now looking through some old boxes. I've got a stack of pictures of family members worth looking through—the ring is on the fingers of some of the men so we might be able to trace the pattern—but nothing concrete about the purpose or powers yet."

Hunter glanced at Syrena and shook his head, watching as her face fell just a little, but she still offered a supportive smile.

Then Phoenix cleared his throat. "But when we were on our way over here, I remembered something from when I was a little kid—something that could be useful. Especially now that I have these pictures in front of me."

Hunter's brow furrowed at that, hope blooming in his chest despite the fact that they'd had nothing but disappointment thus far in their search. "What do you mean?"

Syrena's own brow furrowed as they came up to the train station and slowed.

"When my grandfather died, they forced us to clear out his estate. I took most of it because my father is a deadbeat, my mother was AWOL, and I couldn't tell you what's up with my siblings. I've been emancipated since God knows when. Anyway, in the attic, and in the basement, we found all these old journals. Most of them were so weathered, they were basically unreadable, but some of them were still okay. I read what I could of them, thought nothing of it, you know? I thought . . . well, at the time I thought that it was a story my grandfather had written, a fantasy tale, and I had always loved to read, so I took it. But now I think it might be the documentation of his time as a sign."

Hunter's heart raced. "What do you mean?"

Phoenix sighed. "Listen, it's been years since I read them , but I remember him talking about hunting down a girl, a group of rag-tags, if any of that sounds familiar. I don't know if anything will come of it, so don't get your hopes up. I don't even know if I'll be able to find it in this mess, but I'm going to try. I figure it's better than nothing."

"Anything is better than nothing. And you said there's more than one?"

"Hunter, there's dozens."

"So there has to be something."

"If my family knew anything, it would be in these journals. At least, I hope. I would not want to try to hunt down my father to try to figure out if he knew anything about any of this."

Hunter could hear the disdain in Phoenix's voice over that and his heart ached with sympathy.

In the background, Hunter heard Jupiter yell for Phoenix's attention.

"Listen, I should go help her keep looking. We'll call if we catch any real break-throughs, okay?"

"You got it. Talk soon."

Hunter carefully tucked the phone into his pocket then turned to Syrena. "They have journals from a man that's known to have had his ring. So, it's something."

She squeezed his hand, having not let it go through their entire walk, offering support and stability as they walked up to the ticket counter to retrieve their tickets for their ride, set to board any minute.

"We're going to figure this out, Hunter."

He could only nod and lean down to kiss her temple, while inside his stomach stirred with dread.

Chapter Thirteen: The Train

It didn't take long for Hunter and Syrena to find their seats after boarding the train. The ferry ride had been a couple of hours, but the train would be an overnight adventure, dropping them off in Sussex in the early morning. That meant that they had no choice but to settle in and try to get some sleep while the train chugged along through the English countryside. He took in the landscapes of England, feeling the dichotomy of knowing this was where he was from, and yet, no longer where he belonged at the same time. It filled him with a bittersweet sadness, knowing that he had always loved England for what it was to him but understanding that his home was now in Ireland—was now with the girl dozing softly in the seat across from him.

Hunter glanced at her and he knew that no matter what happened with his parents, he would still leave with her. This wasn't about what he wanted anymore. It was about his purpose in life.

Greater purpose, he thought. *My dad can't argue with that.*

IT WAS SOME HOURS LATER while dozing that Hunter's head bobbed so hard he woke himself up enough to become aware again. He looked up to see Syrena assessing him, something like worry in her eyes. It immediately put him on alert as he sat up straighter.

"Is everything okay, Syrena?" he asked.

"Oh, it's nothing. I didn't mean to worry you." She looked away from him, her cheeks flushing pink with embarrassment.

"Is there something on your mind?" He knew her well enough now to know that she often got that look in her eyes when she'd been deep in thought about something, or when something was bothering her, but she was too nervous to ask or share.

"I just . . . .Well, I feel like there's a reason you don't talk about this if you don't want to." She still wouldn't look at him.

"No, come on. What's going on?" A soft smile graced his lips at her shyness. How beautiful she was.

"Well, you're always so open with us about how important family is. You tell us to stay close, to reach out, all that stuff. But I've noticed that you don't really talk about your family. Earlier, you seemed really anxious about heading home now, it just seems like . . . it seems like there might be more there. I was wondering why."

Hunter looked away from her and out the window of the train. It had started to rain.

"You don't have to tell me. It's none of my business," she said softly, tucking her feet up beneath her in her seat.

"No, I don't mind." He turned back toward her and offered her a slight smile. "I trust you, Syrena. It's just that I've never had anyone pay such attention before. This connection we have . . . I can't explain it."

He quickly got to his feet, switching to sit next to her, then held her hand in his, pressing his lips tenderly to the back of it. He reveled in the sweet smile she rewarded him with. Even with her touch and smile, though, his anxiety had risen at the thought of trying to speak about all this, to explain it to her, to bring her on the inside of it all.

"We had a falling out," he stated simply. That seemed like a good enough place to start. "They wanted me to be something that I wasn't."

"What did they want?" She was studying him as he spoke, taking in all his anxiety and discomfort. He didn't understand her compassion, the kindness that she held for him.

"They wanted me to be a doctor, to take over the family foundation in my dad's place when the time came." The anxiety was being overrun by anger now, and the words were flying out of him faster than he could filter or stop them. "They just didn't understand that I wanted to be something different, that I had different dreams for myself than they had for me."

"What did you want to do?"

Despite the last year that they'd spent together, their connection, their common understanding, Hunter suddenly felt shy at the thought of sharing his innermost desires with her. He knew that she wouldn't laugh, but so many others had that the fear was deep rooted in him and he worried. He had stopped sharing his dreams with the world a long time ago, and to remove that blocker was a difficult task. But Syrena was the one person that seemed to understand him to his core, and if there was anyone in the world that would understand this part of him, it would be her.

"Ever since I was a young boy, I have always loved to find lost treasures, the remains of civilizations that have been lost for centuries."

She smiled as she placed her hand on his arm. She waited quietly for him to continue, not pressuring him, and it put him more at ease.

"It would've been my choice to do something with that. Something with adventure or a story to go with it." He chuckled. "It seems silly to say as an adult, you know?"

"Yet you seem to have found a way to do just that, haven't you?" she said softly.

At that, he looked at her—truly looked at her—and he realized that perhaps he had. Perhaps, for the first time, he understood that it wasn't such a silly wish after all.

Syrena slid her hand down his arm until their hands met, until she was able to thread her fingers through his and close them, locking them together. "Do you believe in fate, Hunter?"

He nodded slightly. He had always believed in the mystical and the unexplained. He believed that they all had a specific purpose to complete while they were alive. He still hadn't figured out his purpose—especially with the confusion regarding what being a sign was—but he knew that it had something to do with Syrena. Even if it didn't, he knew that with her was where he belonged, no matter what.

"I do. My dad always used to say that fate is a power that is supposed to determine, in advance, the way things will happen." Hunter thought it was funny in a way, how his dad had been the one to teach him about fate, then try to deter him from following something that he now knew felt so much like it.

Syrena smiled sadly. "It reminds me of what my father used to say about destiny. He said it's the outcome that is bound to come. There is nothing you can do to change your destiny. It's written in the stars, and they will lead you on your path through life."

Hunter smiled and pulled Syrena into his arms, hugging her gently.

"You don't know how long I have been waiting for you," she murmured softly. "I thought I would never find someone like you. You have such a pure heart. I'm glad that it was you."

He pulled back slightly and looked into her eyes. He had been searching for her for so long that he wasn't sure if this was actually real, even now. He didn't want to get his hopes up again. "Yes, I do. I have been searching for you my whole life. I just figured that a princess would never fall for a guy like me."

Hunter looked away sadly as she studied him, his cheeks pinking after his confession. There were so many emotions swimming within him, the stress of this whole journey catching up with him.

"Hunter, any girl would be lucky to be with you. You have a wonderful heart and an amazing soul to match. I have been searching for years for someone like you. I was about to give up but then I met you. I knew it was you the moment I looked into your eyes. My mother used to say that you can see into a person's soul by looking into their eyes. I never understood what she meant until now."

He smiled up at her as she moved closer, against his side, then wrapped her arms around his neck. They studied each other's faces for a long time, and he knew by the way her eyes flitted around that she was trying to read his emotions. His ability to hide his emotions from the world had been perfected years ago, but he wanted Syrena to know the real him, and he was okay with that. He didn't want to hide the real him from her. Hunterneeded to know that she liked him for who he was, not who she thought he was.

"Thank you, Syrena. I've dreamt about you since I was twelve years old. I've wished my whole life that I would find the girl from my dreams. I'm so glad that I found you."

"I feel it too, Hunter. I can't explain the connection I feel with you. I feel safe for the first time in a long time."

He studied her quietly, glad she felt the connection too. This was the first time in years that he felt comfortable being himself. He didn't want this journey home to close him off again. He hoped she knew that whatever this journey did to him had nothing to do with her.

"I'm grateful you welcomed me into your home and your life. You mean a lot to me, Syrena."

She stared down at his chest before looking up into his eyes. There were so many emotions there that it scared him. The fear crept back in again. *What if he couldn't fulfill his promise? What if they traveled all this way and came up with nothing?*

"You have given me hope again," she said softly.

He smiled as he pulled her against his chest and hoped she couldn't hear his heart racing.

"We better head to bed," she said. "Long day tomorrow."

He nodded, his chin bumping the top of her head as he did so. He didn't understand how he became so lucky to have found her, but he didn't want to let her go. He held her for a long time before slowly pulling back. She stared up into his eyes for a moment before he leaned down and pressed his lips to hers, savoring it when she smiled against him.

"Goodnight, Syrena," he said softly as he pulled away.

"Goodnight, Hunter."

She smiled up at him before softly kissing his cheek.

Hunter made to get up and return to his seat across from her, but she locked her arm around his, pulling him back down next to her and resting her head on his shoulder. Despite the anxiety swirling inside of him, Hunter smiled, pressing a kiss to the top of her hair before resting his cheek there. As he laid against her, his mind finally quieted, and he was able to drift off to sleep.

Chapter Fourteen: Family Reunion

Sitting in front of his parents' house in a taxi the next morning, Hunter's entire body broke out in a cold sweat. He'd been nervous about things before—nervous about trying to find Syrena, nervous about breaking the curse, even nervous about mundane things before that—but never in his life had he been so nervous that his entire body grew clammy from it.

"We don't have to do this," Syrena said softly from behind him, ever supportive, ever on his side.

It made his heart swell—and he almost took her up on it.

Instead, he sighed. "No. We came all this way, and we need whatever information they have about what's happening with all of this." He let out a long exhale. "Besides," he turned to look at her and grinned, "they should get to know the girl I'm dating right?"

Syrena's cheeks flushed as she smiled back at him. Then, after squeezing his hand once, she turned and got out of the car.

With another brief hesitation, Hunter followed her.

In another few moments, they'd retrieved their bags from the trunk and walked up the concrete path to the front door. It looked, for all intent and purposes, exactly the way that it had when Hunter left last year. It was the same faded shade of navy blue with equally faded off-white shutters, the same walkway that his mother had spent too much money on and his dad had yelled about for a week, the same yard that was always properly trimmed thanks to the gardeners his dad had hired because he was always too busy to cut it himself, the same overflowing gardens in the front of the house with properly seasonal flowers–not a single wilted petal or weed in sight. His mother's dedication to her flowers was a stark contrast to his dad's inattention to the rest of the yard, her love for those blossoms rivaling her love for most other hobbies or activities.

It made him as sad as it did relieved. Had he stayed, he knew, he would have stagnated:never growing, never changing—predictable, reliable, and bored senseless.

"Ready?" Syrena prompted softly, pulling his attention back to the task at hand.

He cleared his throat, giving the yard one more cursory sweep, then nodded. He knocked twice, then stepped back, allowing room for the door to swing toward him when his parents came.

Only they didn't.

They waited thirty seconds, then a minute, with no response.

Hunter glanced to the driveway, then to Syrena and raised his hand to knock again.

This time, he heard his dad yell from inside.

"Whoever it is, now isn't a good time. I'm in the middle of a meeting—"

His dad's voice cut off as the door swung open and their eyes met—the same set of gray irises, reflecting back at each other. His dad's had more wrinkles around them now, his hair a little grayer than it was when he'd left, but it was still unmistakably his dad .

Into the phone at his ear, he said, "I'll have to call you back," then let the device slip away from his head to his side.

"Hey, Dad," Hunter said, the words feeling foreign on his tongue.

Hayden Monroe sized his son up from feet to hair then back again before his eyes flicked to Syrena and did the same.

"Ivy," Hayden called into the house. "Ivy!"

"What?" Hunter heard his mother call back from within the house—most likely from her favorite chair in the living room. "Who is it?"

"You're going to want to see this for yourself."

"Hayden, I don't have time for games right now. I'm in the middle of making a shopping list and I've a million other things—"

"Ivy, darling, I wouldn't interrupt you if it weren't important."

Hayden's eyes were back on his son's now—but something cold had taken over the initial shock that lived there when he'd first opened the door. It forced Hunter to swallow thickly, that anxiety from the taxi compounding within him. His previous fears—of how his dad reacted, of how his *mother* would take his return—began swirling anew in his head.

What had he been thinking just dropping in on them like this? Who just dropped *in on family after a year of no contact? Crazy people, that was who.*

Hunter cleared his throat as he heard his mother's footsteps approach.

"Who is it, Hayden, really? I have so much to—"

Ivy's words died on her tongue as she rounded her husband and glanced out to the front walk, taking in her son standing there.

"Hi, Mom," Hunter said, his words thick with emotion as he took his mom in—the same apron she always wore when she was in the kitchen, even when she didn't cook, her glasses on top of her head despite the fact that she needed them to read, her perfume, the same as it had always been.

He was overcome by emotions he wasn't prepared for. Hurt, anger, frustration—he'd been ready for those. But to be homesick? To miss them? He wasn't ready for that.To have them standing next to one another on their front porch, peering at him , his mother's hand over her mouth, eyes full of tears as she looked him over, he suddenly couldn't swallow around the thump in his throat.

"Oh, Hunter," she choked out, finally breaking the tension between all of them as she stepped forward and threw her arms around him, pulling him tight, the way she always had.

"Mom," he said into her hair, hugging her just as tightly.

Over her head, he watched as his dad crossed his arms over his chest, a scowl playing on his lips. Hunter merely closed his eyes. That was something to be dealt with in a moment. For now, he reveled in the hug from his mother, the love only a mother could give to her son.

ONCE IVY FINALLY RELEASED her son, Hunter and Syrena were ushered into the living room, where Hunter and Syrena promptly gave them the watered-down version of everything that had happened to them in the last year, starting with Hunter leaving home. The story was egged on by Ivy, who Hunter knew was just happy to have him home. How much of it she believed, he didn't know, but he was grateful that she didn't seem angry. She listened, she laughed, she nodded.

"When Luna said that people were coming for us, we knew we needed more information," Syrena said softly as the story came to a close.

Hunter nodded. "Those of us known as the signs, have no idea what role we play, and with Syrena's parents gone, it's our job to help her figure out what she's supposed to do. So, we thought we would track it down to the source, to the people that gave us those signs in the first place." Hunter shrugged, his full attention on his dad.

His dad did nothing but sit and watch them, arms crossed, eyes flickering back and forth between them as they recounted their story.

"Well, what a story that is," Ivy said. "Don't you think, Hayden?"

Hunter's dad said nothing, just continued to watch the two of them on the couch.

Even long after they'd finished and Ivy had disappeared into the kitchen to make them a snack, his dad continued to watch them in silence, scrutinizing.

At some point during this, Syrena reached over and took Hunter's hand, giving his fingers a comforting squeeze. Whether it was entirely for him or for her as well, he didn't know, but he returned the gesture, hoping that she was doing okay. He wished he'd debriefed her more on his family—on his dad, his dad's quiet anger.

It wasn't until his mother had returned to the room that his dad spoke for the first time since summoning his mother to the door.

"So, explain this to me," he said, settling a hard gaze on Hunter. "You expect me to believe that you set off to find the girl you were dreaming about, you actually *found* her, and in the process, you discovered that she has magical powers? And that, somehow, you also have them because of a family heirloom that's been passed down for generations?"

Hunter nodded.

"An heirloom that *I* had, and never experienced any of these...symptoms from?"

"Yes, Mr. Monroe. Everything Hunter has told you, that I've said, has been the truth," Syrena said, smiling softly at him.

"This is between me and my son," Hayden snapped at her.

"Don't talk to her like that," Hunter warned, his voice low in his throat.

Hayden raised an eyebrow but said nothing further on the matter. Instead, he pressed on. "What do you think I would know about some magical earring, Hunter?"

Hunter shrugged. "I honestly wouldn't know where to begin. The history of it? Who made it? How it was passed down? Anything would be helpful at this point, since we know nothing."

Hayden's responding laugh was not one of kindness. "It's just an earring, Hunter. Your grandfather gave it to me, and his father before him."

Hunter swallowed his growl of frustration. "Okay, well, does it have a certificate or something timestamping it? Saying who's owned it previously?"

His dad rolled his eyes. "This is a ridiculous quest you're on, son. When are you going to stop playing pretend and smarten up?"

"Pretending?" Hunter said, looking at Syrena, whose eyes were wide in shock.

"You've thrown your tantrum, proved your point by bringing the girl here. But enough is enough. You need to smarten up and settle down."

"Hayden," Ivy scolded, but his dad shook off the warning.

"This is the last I'll hear about this fantasy nonsense. You'll send her away or you'll both leave and leave us to our lives. No son of mine will disgrace this family playing these...games." Hayden sneered at Syrena, then rose from his chair and stalked from the room.

Hunter watched his dad go, his blood boiling but his mind surprisingly calm. He had expected this, he reminded himself. He had known how his dad felt about this.

His sigh was deep, exhausted.

Chapter Fifteen: Nothing but Disappointment

"I can talk to him," Ivy said over a lunch of sandwiches she'd made in the kitchen.

Despite his dad's request, his mother had refused to let them leave, instead, forcing food upon them and encouraging them to leave their stuff in Hunter's old bedroom with a promise that one night wouldn't kill any of them.

"You traveled so far to be here," she'd said. "Please stay. I'm sure he knows more than he's letting on. If this... thing is really as big as you say it is, there's no way that was passed to him without any of the history that was attached to it."

Syrena shrugged softly. "Actually, we've run into that with all of the signs so far. A lot of the history has been lost. From what I've been able to infer, the signs haven't been called together in over a generation, so we're getting secondhand accounts at this point. It's possible that all of our parents had no idea of the power they possessed. Even my mother failed to pass her knowledge on to me before she passed."

Ivy's eyes saddened at that. "I'm very sorry for your loss, Syrena," she said softly.

Syrena lowered her head in thanks.

"I doubt Dad knows anything, or retained any of it if he did, at any point."

Ivy sighed. "Don't be so hard on him, Hunter. This would be a lot to take in for anyone."

"Don't defend him on this," Hunter said, more harshly than he'd intended, but he didn't apologize. His dad didn't deserve to be defended, not after his behavior had driven Hunter away a year ago and it seemed even that had done nothing to motivate him to change. Had losing him really not been enough to make him consider that perhaps he had been in the wrong? Even after all this time, did he still consider Hunter to be the one that had made the mistakes here?.

"Hunter," his mother said in a tone only a mother could use.

"What?" he said. "He'd rather lose me again than entertain for a second that anything I've gone through in the last year is true."

Ivy sighed. "He's a hard headed man, Hunter. Even I'm having some difficulty with it."

Hunter just looked at her for a long moment before returning to his sandwich.

Syrena cut in, and Hunter knew she was trying to further defuse the tension. "We're just really at a loss right now as to what to do next. We broke the curse, but now there's this impending threat that we know very little about, so we're just trying to get any information we can. We're grasping at straws. We thought coming here would give us something."

Ivy nodded. "I'm sorry that it didn't."

"So are we," Hunter muttered.

That effectively ended the conversation. The rest of the meal was spent in silence.

HUNTER'S DAD DIDN'T come out of his study for the remainder of the day, and Ivy told them that if he wasn't making an appearance then he wouldn't know they were there to spend the night. Awkwardly, they managed to watch a movie together. Syrena talked to Ivy about her childhood and upbringing at the manor. Briefly, they talked more in detail about the curse, and what little they knew about their powers.

Still, Hunter could tell that his mother was at a loss about what to do with the information they presented. More than that, he was angry—angry at his dad for the way he dismissed Syrena, angry at his parents that they couldn't see that what he was doing meant something, and angry at himself that he had dragged Syrena all the way back to England, just to end knowing nothing more. He felt like he'd led them all astray, searching for answers about the signs that he'd let them all down.

It didn't help that he hadn't heard anything from Phoenix or Jupiter either, only driving home the fact that so far, these trips had been a complete waste of everyone's time.

Frustration welled in Hunter until he stood up abruptly, drawing both his mother and Syrena's attention.

"If you'll excuse me."

He left without another word , positive or otherwise.

HE WAS SURE THAT IT was stupid to even bother, knew that it probably wouldn't produce a different answer, but his right hand came up to the door before he could think twice about it. Rapping hard, before his left hand turned the door knob, he didn't wait for an answer.

His dad's eyes were full of fury when they lifted to him in the doorway, as if he knew before he'd stepped in, who would be on the other side. Perhaps he had known—a year would not erase the way his footsteps sounded on the hallway floor, he decided.

"I thought I told you both to leave."

"When are you going to realize that I don't do what you tell me to, anymore?" Hunter hissed, shutting the door behind him so that his mother and Syrena wouldn't hear them in the living room.

"I never thought I would raise a son who was so disrespectful," Hayden said, standing so hard, his chair squeaked back across the hardwoods.

"It wouldn't be disrespectful if you had half a mind to listen to the words that came out of my mouth, to listen to the things that I wanted or needed."

When he'd come in here, this wasn't the conversation he'd intended to have. Perhaps he didn't know what conversation he intended to have, but he knew that there was more to be said—a lot more—and this was somewhere to start.

"I need to know whatever you know about this earring, Dad. It could mean saving her, saving Ireland, saving all of us."

Hayden shook his head. "You're living in a fantasy, Hunter. A story world. You need to grow up and realize that those things—dreams and hopes and *love*—don't pay the bills, don't keep food on the table and a roof over your head."

"Maybe life isn't always about just those things. Maybe dreams and hopes and *love,* as you put it, are more important." Hunter sneered at his dad.

"You don't know what you're talking about. You don't know anything. You're just a child."

"Then enlighten me. What am I missing, Dad? Huh?" Hunter threw his arms out to the sides. "That's literally all I've come here to learn. I just need to know what this is all about so I can go home and protect the woman I love. Tell me, would you not do the same for Mom?"

"I *did* do the same for Mom!" Hayden hissed, eyes full of fury as he stared at his son.

Hunter flinched back at his dad's words, watched as what he'd said settled into his dad's own face.

Hayden sat back down, then sighed heavily. "I *did*."

"What do you mean?"

Hayden looked at Hunter for a long time, looked to his ear, then back to his face. "When your grandfather gave me that earring, when I was a boy, he told me a grand story. A story about a girl, a light, and an adventure to protect people. It sounded like something out of a story book."

"It sounds familiar." Hunter crossed his arms.

Hayden's returned laugh was humorless. "About the time that your mother got pregnant with you, that earring started to burn a hole in my ear. It hurt, it was heavy, it was ridiculous. And the *dreams...*"

Hunter's heart was nearly beating out of his chest.

"I thought it was stress. I'd just taken my position at the foundation, a new baby on the way, the move, the marriage. It was all so much. But when I mentioned it to your grandfather, he said that it was the call. That I had to answer it. That if I didn't go, it would be the fate of the world in my hands. That the lives lost would be on my conscience."

"Did you go?" Hunter asked.

Hayden scoffed. "I took the earring off and threw it in a drawer. To run away? To leave my family? Leave the foundation? For something I didn't even know existed? It felt like a cosmic joke."

"And what happened?"

"Nothing." Hayden chuckled. "Absolutely nothing."

But Hunter's mind was already racing. He'd ignored the call... and Anabelle had died. Perhaps from sickness, yes, but she died. And none of the other signs had shown up either. They hadn't stayed together and...

The curse.

Perhaps it was a stretch... or perhaps it wasn't. With something as convoluted as this, it was all connected.

"The girl you were supposed to protect was Syrena's mother," Hunter said. "She's dead. And Syrena was cursed because of it. The other signs never showed up to protect them and she died."

Hunter was almost satisfied by the flash that crossed through his dad's eyes: fear. Guilt.

Perhaps it was wrong to pin this on him...but it still felt good after his dad's expectations, when he'd failed to fulfill what his dad said was his duty.

"That isn't on me," Hayden said softly.

"Isn't it?" Hunter hissed. "Why didn't you go?"

"I had a life."

"You could have come back to it."

"Could I have? Look at you, tied up in this forever." Hayden sneered.

"I chose this, chose her."

"And I *didn't*."

They stared at each other, challenging each other, neither one willing to back down—until Hunter sighedand righted himself.

"I just need to know what you know. Before more people die."

Hayden shook his head. "I don't know anything. Your grandfather simply told me that the earring would give me the strength I needed to save her. It was my job to always make sure she was protected."

Hunter's brows furrowed. "But Anabelle wasn't cursed. She didn't need to be healed."

"I don't know, Hunter, that's what he said. He said when he was called to Ireland, his job was to heal her through the worst of it, and I was to do the same. My duty was to keep her well, then pass the earring on to the next generation. I did my part."

"Half of your part," Hunter said with half a glare. "Though you almost stopped that from happening as well."

"What was I to do? Support you in running off on a whim?"

"Yes," Hunter yelled. "Especially if that's what Grandpa did and what you were *supposed* to do!"

"I can't talk about this anymore with you. I need you to get the girl and get out of my house if you continue to believe this... this... garbage."

Hunter looked down at his dad, rage building in his chest. But he turned toward the study door instead and gripped the handle. As he made to leave the room, he turned one more time to his dad.

"Her name is Syrena."

He made sure to slam the door behind him as he left.

Chapter Sixteen: Returning to Tara

His mother gave them money to fly back to Ireland. He told her they couldn't take it, but she insisted it was the least she could do, especially after the way his dad had reacted. Their send-off was anticlimactic, but it broke his heart nonetheless.

"Remember to come visit me," Ivy said into his shirt as she hugged him tight. "I've missed you."

"I'll come when I can, Mom."

"At least write. Call. Something." She pulled back, tears running down her face, then said, "And be very careful. I don't know what you're mixed up in, Hunter, but you better make it out alive."

"I'll do my best," he said with a soft kiss to her cheek.

Then they were off—a taxi ride to the airport and a plane ride home.

By the time they stumbled into the manor that evening, Hunter was so wiped out emotionally, physically, and mentally that he wanted nothing more than to lay in bed and sleep for ten years. Instead, he was greeted with a steaming mug of hot coffee almost as soon as he stepped into the foyer.

"Drink up," Phoenix said. "These journals aren't going to read themselves."

Hunter did everything he could to swallow his groan as he rubbed his face with his free hand, then sipped from the mug in the other. Syrena did the same. She looked so tired she was practically swaying on her feet.

"Have you figured anything out?" Hunter asked as they followed Phoenix to the study.

"Not much beyond what we already know. Dreams, charms, White Light, pretty girls." Nix shot Syrena a wink and she smiled at him.

Hunter rolled his eyes. "I basically got the same information from my dad—except that he refused to follow the call."

Both Jupiter and Nix turned to him. He'd filled Syrena in on the flight, and she'd drawn some of the same conclusions he had, along with some of the same what-ifs.

"He *refused*?" Jupiter asked incredulously.

Hunter nodded.

"What does that even mean?" Nix pushed.

"The signs were called, but he took the earring out, threw it in a drawer and ignored the nagging until it went away. He didn't come."

Nix whistled. "That's one way to deal with it."

Jupiter nodded in agreement.

"So, I hope you guys have better news than that."

"Well, we're one generation behind, but we haven't got much to go on yet, like I said. So... get reading."

Hunter downed the rest of his coffee, grabbed a journal off the stack on the desk, and settled into one of the armchairs to read.

Syrena, though, wandered over to the window and peered outside, taking in the setting sun outside.

They were all silent for a long time, until Syrena's gasp filled the room, followed by the clatter and smash of the cup she'd been holding.

Hunter was at her side in an instant.

"Syrena? What is it? What's wrong?"

Her eyes were wide with fear, unfocused, as she collapsed into his arms.

Jupiter and Phoenix were next to them in a minute, Phoenix on Syrena's other side, as he helped to lift a now dazed Syrena into one of the chairs. Jupiter, however, was looking out the window.

"Guys," she called, her tone panicked. "Whatever we aren't finding, we're going to want to work to find it faster. Because I think we're running out of time."

Phoenix and Hunter shared a look over Syrena's now unconscious body, then ran to the window to look at what was outside.

In the garden, Hunter watched as half the roses wilted and died, a slow creeping death that worked its way toward the house. At the far end of the garden, an apparition stood— similar to Luna, but different.

Instead of gold, the apparition shone black as midnight. As the three of them stared at it, it stared back. It didn't move toward the house, or try to communicate. It just watched. Then, once it made eye contact with each of them, as if it was sure it had been seen, it turned and disappeared into the woods at the edge of the garden and vanished.

Jupiter turned to the rest of them, eyes as wide as the moon now shining in the sky.

"This is about to get a lot worse for us, isn't it?" she asked softly.

Hunter's face was solemn as he turned back to Syrena laying on the couch.

What were they going to do now?

READ NEXT

THE KEEPER OF THE LIGHT SERIES
BOOK THREE
AUSTYN'S CHOICE

AUSTYN'S CHOICE

THE KEEPER OF THE LIGHT SERIES BOOK THREE

Austyn Martin stood on the edge of the Cliffs of Tara, the cold wind whipping through his hair, carrying with it the salty tang of the Atlantic. It was hard to believe that just months ago, he was a solitary figure, lost in the shadows of his own family's expectations. Here, amidst the beauty of Ireland, he had found a ragtag group of friends who had become his chosen family—-each of them battling their own demons, yet united by a bond stronger than blood.

The bracelet on his wrist felt heavier now, a constant reminder of the secrets he had unearthed during his time abroad. It glimmered in the fading light, its intricate designs whispering tales of his ancestry and the truth that lay buried under layers of family lies. With each passing day, he felt the weight of his heritage press down on him, urging him to confront the past he had always run from.

As he turned away from the cliffs, memories flooded back—laughter shared over pints of stout, late-night confessions by the fire, and the warmth of their unwavering support as they faced the encroaching darkness together. But those moments were now tainted with the knowledge that the battle was not over. His friends needed him, and the darkness they faced was inching closer, threatening to consume everything they had built together.

His heart raced at the thought of returning to America. Would they understand his transformation? Would they recognize the person he had become, or would they see only the outsider they had always known? He clenched his fists, the bracelet digging into his skin, a silent vow to uncover the truth behind its origins and to confront his family about their secrets—-secrets that had kept him shackled in loneliness for far too long.

Don't miss out!

Visit the website below and you can sign up to receive emails whenever Kristen Cole publishes a new book. There's no charge and no obligation.

https://books2read.com/r/B-A-VDHRB-GAKKF

BOOKS 2 READ

Connecting independent readers to independent writers.

About the Author

Kristen Cole is a writer from a small town in Arizona. As a young girl, she dreamed of becoming two things; a teacher and an author. Now years later, she is making her dreams come true. She was a reading, writing, and daydreamer in high school who turned her dreams into reality. She went into the field of education after high school with a passion for teaching. She now splits her time between teaching 4th grade and working on her next novel. She is currently working on book two in The Keeper of the Light series. She writes sweet, fun, adventure packed stories. Her characters are clever, fearless, and searching for who they are meant to be and never apologize for being different.